The
Active-Enzyme
Lemon-Freshened
Junior High School
Witch

The
Active-Enzyme
Lemon-Freshened
Junior High School
Witch

E. W. HILDICK

Illustrated by Iris Schweitzer

A YEARLING BOOK

Published by
Dell Publishing Co., Inc.
1 Dag Hammarskjold Plaza
New York, New York 10017

Yearling ® TM 913705, Dell Publishing Co., Inc.
ISBN: 0-440-43147-6
Reprinted by arrangement with Doubleday & Company, Inc.
Printed in the United States of America
Fifth Dell Printing—May 1979
MPC

To Fenella and Caroline,
in whose house this book was started.
And to Penny and Sasha,
in whose garden it was finished.
And also to Giovanna and Alessandra,
whose witchcraft has a range
of at least a thousand miles.

Contents

The
Active-Enzyme
Lemon-Freshened
Junior High School
Witch

CHAPTER 1

"Who is this that comes?"

I first discovered I was a Witch with the Power to Conjure Up the Dead when I was but 12 that time (last month) on vacation up in West Salem. It was not THE Salem up in Massachusetts; it was one of the Salems up near the New York/Connecticut border. But borders are powerfully Magic Places and the Witchcraft was real enough, as you will Surely Find if you dare to Smile at these my Words (or even Look at them without Permission).

EXTRACT FROM
THE MAGICAL WORKBOOK OF ARIADNE ATROPOS ARACHNE
(ALIAS ALISON JANE VERONICA MCNAIR)

It's always the same with people like Alison McNair. It's not just that one thing leads to another. That happens all the time with anybody. Like running too fast, then falling, then getting up . . . a good thing, a bad thing, a fairly good thing . . . and so on. But with people like Alison it's more cumulative—with the thing that is led to being like the thing that led to it, only better, much better. Or of course worse, much worse.

In Alison's case the direction was usually worse. Much, much worse. And this was because she was so impatient, so eager to be getting results. (For instance, that Witch Name of hers. Most people just adopt one Witch Name when they start up in the business. But not Alison. Oh, no! It had to be three for her. Three A's at that—so that every time she saw a car with the AAA sticker it reminded her of her supernatural powers and gave her a kick.)

Anyway, there we have Alison. On the outside: a thin-faced girl, wolf-faced almost, with big brown fiercely brooding eyes—and yet with thick red hair that was altogether too bright to go with such a face. On the inside, the same mixture: a serious girl—very serious for her age—but impatient.

And here we have the situation, with one thing leading to another, right at the start of the summer vacation: a bug, a cough, a sniffle, a headache, a fever, a sweat, a rash, the measles. With a brother of the bug getting to work on Alison's kid sister Jeannie (seven) about a week later, so that when Alison was sweating it out, Jeannie was starting with a cough; and when Alison was just beginning to feel better, Jeannie was getting to feel terrible and letting everyone know it. In fact, she made it so hard for Alison to enjoy her own convalescence that the older girl became twice as impatient as usual. She became so anxious to be up and out of the way of the coughing and groaning and tossing and turning that

were going on in the bed across the room that her
recovery was slowed down, and at the end of the third
week the sisters' measles were practically neck and neck
and spot for spot. Alison should have known it would
turn out like this: a girl her age, with all her experience.
She should have learned long since that (especially in
illness) if there is one thing a thing hates when it's doing
its thing of leading to another thing, it is being hustled.

But Alison never did learn.

On the very day of her Great Discovery she was still
trying to push things along.

"If only there was a television set in this—this *her-
mitage!*" she groaned as she sat up in bed, her hands
clasped around her knees, her body gently rocking.

"*We* couldn't look at it anyway," said Jeannie. "Could
we, Sylvie?"

Sylvie was her walking/talking/wetting doll—her best.
Or rather, her *ex*-walking doll, after Alison's experiments
some months previously to see if they could get Sylvie to
run.

Alison glared across as the younger girl fussed with
the cripple, pretending that it too was falling ill with
measles.

"Yaaarr!" bleated the doll.

This was supposed to mean either yes or no according
to which way you got its fool head to wag. As a result of
another of Alison's experiments (always conducted with
the full approval of the "mother" until they started
going wrong), Sylvie's head had had to be refixed as
rigid as any old-fashioned wooden doll's, although even

Jeannie admitted that it *would* have been marvelous if Alison *had* been able to get it to say "Happy New Year!"

"What d'you mean, *we* couldn't look at television even if we had one?" asked Alison. "Why couldn't we?"

She knew perfectly well why not. But she'd figured it might lead to a good argument. Even a row. Anything better than this—this *languishing* around in a strange bedroom, with nothing you wanted ever being at hand.

"Because the doctor said so. About our eyes. Didn't he, Sylvie?"

"Yaaarr!" mewed the stupid puppet between the sheets.

"The doctor!" growled Alison. "That peasant! What does he know about it? Why, he—he's only a veterinarian. Really. He is. Just a veterinarian. That's all they have out here in the country. You know that."

"He—" Jeannie turned and looked at her sister. She had big brown eyes, too, but they were softly serious, not fiercely so, and her face was round and soon split up into smiles and was more in keeping with the same bright redness of hair. "You're joking me again!"

Alison had to smile, in spite of her boredom.

"How many more times? You don't *joke* someone—you kid them. Joking is just joking. You just joke. . . . It's intransitive," she added grandly.

"Oh—I see!"

"You don't see at all. You *say* you see, but you don't. You—"

Alison stopped. This talk of seeing had reminded her of the television they didn't have, and now she had an idea.

"Jeannie," she said, "we'll make our own puppet television show. Just pass Sylvie over to me. Come *on*. You want her to be a star, don't you? With her own series? . . . Well, then . . ."

And so the hustling began again. With the usual results.

There was no careful planning. There was no *thinking* things over, let alone discussion. The first episode of the "Great New Gripping Series" (as Alison very quickly called it) had to be presented then, that very afternoon, the sooner the better. And it had to be all Alison's own work—everything about it, every line of dialogue, every glimmer of character, every bit of the action—apart from the most humble tasks of assembling the props.

"You see, honey," Alison explained when Jeannie began to inquire about the nature of the plot, "if I let you know what's going to happen, it won't be as interesting, anything *like* as interesting, right?"

"But—"

"Right. So just stop asking questions and hurry along with those socks. I want each of them turning inside and outside until they make two little chubby bundles."

These were some white knee-length nylon socks of Alison's. They were destined, when they'd been pummeled into the right lengths and degree of plumpness, to play the parts of Buffy and Bobby, Sylvie's younger brother and sister, six-year-old twins, cute, lovable, but accident-prone, with a long future of illnesses, injuries, knockings-down, beatings-up, and kidnapings in front of them. That's how Alison had them figured, anyway, just as she had made instant plans for a new king-size tube of toothpaste ("Clarinda, a beautiful but aging model with a terrible past"), a hairbrush with black bristles and a brown leather back ("Romanov, a sinister monk from Siberia, over here on a secret mission"), and a can of Muguet talcum powder ("Sylvie's old grandmother, a Frenchwoman from New Orleans, who suffers from dandruff").

Alison, in her headlong hurry, could have gone on to build up a cast of hundreds, using every likely-sized object in the room. Probably she would have done so, too, if after settling the talc can's role, she hadn't happened to notice the white comb lying on the floor. Snatched out of the hairbrush in the heat of Romanov's creation, it had gone skiddering over the edge of the marble-topped bedroom washstand and a number of its teeth had been bent out of line in the process.

"Oh, *yes!*" cried Alison, picking it up and plucking at the damaged teeth. "Of *course!*"

Then, telling Jeannie to get herself settled comfortably while the star had the finishing touches put to her makeup, Alison picked up Sylvie and, still holding the comb, bustled off into the next room, a kind of sitting room adjoining the girls' attic bedroom.

"*What* makeup?" demanded Jeannie.

"You'll see," came Alison's voice. Then: "Oh, *darn* the thing!"

"What? What's wrong? Darn what?"

"Never mind. Nothing. You stay right there now—no peeping!"

Alison came back to the room. The rash that encircled her neck was burning fiercely again as she looked around.

"What's wrong? You haven't hurt Sylvie again, have—?"

"Of course I haven't! Be quiet. . . . Ah, yes! Why not?"

Alison snatched up an almost empty toothpaste tube that the other one had been ready to replace, before its TV possibilities as a beautiful but aging model had been recognized.

"Be ready in a sec," said Alison, dashing back into the sitting room in a swirl of green silk nightgown.

Two minutes later, Sylvie had been brought back into the bedroom, her head carefully averted from the viewer, and the first scene was under way.

"Here we have the twins' bedroom," said Alison, indicating the top of her bedside table, which she'd completely cleared by sweeping everything off onto the bed, lamp and all. "And here," she continued, laying the two plumped-up socks side by side in the center of the stage, "are the twins, asleep. See the cute way they lie, the little boy on his back with his knees up, breathing softly, gently blowing one of his stray golden curls this way and that way—"

"I—"

Jeannie was no doubt going to say something about all *she* could see was a pair of socks, but Alison raised her voice a little and gave it more of a singsong rhythm, slightly sinister, the way she sometimes told scary stories at night, in the dark, and Jeannie fell respectfully silent.

"And see the unsuspecting little girl, dreaming gentle dreams, a happy scene, but wait. . . . Who is this that comes?"

Slowly, her back still to Jeannie, Sylvie was propelled into the picture, onto the tabletop, over to the sleeping twins.

"Ah, it is only their big sister Sylvie, come to kiss them goodnight. See, she stoops to the little boy; see, she stoops to the little girl. . . . But—but what is this? Why does she continue to stoop there? Does she see something on the little girl's pillow? And why does she shudder so, and make strange noises?"

Here, Alison got the stooping, shuddering doll to bleat out its "Yaaarr!" sound, which, thanks to the buildup she'd given it, sounded so weird that it made Jeannie start slightly.

"Oh, no!" then gasped Alison, still in her ghost-story voice. "It cannot be! It *must* not be! But alas, my goodness, oh heavens, oh horrors, it IS!"

"Whu-what?" whispered Jeannie.

"Sylvie," intoned Alison, in a loud, resonant voice, "good, sweet, kind, big sister Sylvie—is nothing else—but—a—*vampire!* SEE!"

Whereupon she turned Sylvie's face to the audience (for the first time since she'd re-entered the bedroom, remember)—which is when Jeannie gave a loud long lung-draining lusty scream.

And no wonder.

As if the sight of the two new sharp ivory teeth, projecting one from each side of the familiar mouth, usually set in a rosebud simper, wasn't horrible enough, there was the thick blob of toothpaste that was helping to keep them fixed there. And although mere ordinary white toothpaste would no doubt have had a similar scream-provoking effect, with its suggestion of evil frothing, *this* had to be the kind with a bright red ribbon of fluoride running through it.

"*Now* what's wrong?" demanded the producer, having the presence of mind to put the offending doll behind her back. "It's only a play."

"I—I don't like this play. And what"—here Jeannie's voice tailed off nervously—"what did you do to Sylvie?"

"How do you *know* you don't like it? It's hardly even started."

"I—I wanted a nice funny one. Where there's a family, and the children get into trouble and—"

"Well, so the children *are* getting into trouble."

"And you said Sylvie was going to be the star and have lots of adventures—"

"And so she is."

"Well, she *can't* be then, if she's a horrid vampire. She—"

"*Why* can't she be? She can't help being a vampire. That's the funny thing. Like the woman who's a witch in that series you *like!*"

"Yes, but—"

"Oh well, have it your own way. Make your own TV show up if you think you know everything."

Now what Alison really meant was that she'd suddenly realized her sister was right—that there was, when she came to think of it, nothing very funny about a vampire series. But Alison would sooner have suffered a visit from a real bloodsucking monster herself than make such a confession to Jeannie of all people.

So, with a sniff and a shrug of her shoulders, she tossed the doll back to Jeannie, and Jeannie instinctively caught it, hugging it to her chest, completely forgetting the look on its face the last time she'd seen it.

"Poor Sylvie!" she murmured. "*You* don't wanna be a wicked old—"

And then Jeannie screamed again as she felt one of the comb teeth pricking into her neck, where it remained, held there by part of the blob of toothpaste, even after she'd hurled the doll, with yet another scream, right across the room.

"*What on earth goes on?*"

Mrs. McNair was at the door, staring at the doll that had landed at her feet and prodding it gingerly with the end of the golf club she was carrying.

CHAPTER 2

The View That Beckoned,
the Book That Clutched . . .

Later that afternoon—after she had apologized to her
mother for being the cause of the screaming, and had
refused to apologize to her sister on the ground that the
scaring had not been intended, and had apologized to
her mother for refusing to apologize to her sister, and
had then apologized to her sister but with crossed
fingers—Alison sat by the window of the upstairs sitting
room, being GOOD, and HURT, and CALM, and
PATIENT.

Patient? *Alison McNair?*

Well, it was an act, of course. It was being patient
writ large. She was too fully conscious of being each of
these things for them to be normal. She was working at
them. Hard.

And since they were all passive things, not requiring
forward movement, all her headlong spirit went into
making them swell and outgrow themselves.

So being GOOD meant blinking gently under a
smooth, smooth forehead, and forgiving, sweetly and
generously, that cowardly malicious fink in the next
room—that younger sister of hers now smugly snuffling

over her idiot doll—that traitor who had deliberately
exaggerated her alarm in order to get her, the gentle
Alison, into trouble.

And being HURT meant biting—oh, so secretly!—at
her upper lip while bravely smiling, like (she stretched
her neck up and turned from the window to catch her
reflection in the mirror on the opposite wall) *that*, but
with her head just a little more dipped, *thus*.

Being CALM was one of her favorites. For this, she
lifted her chin, not too high (that would have taken her
into her PROUD face), and she smiled a faint smile,
fainter than the HURT smile, perfectly balanced at the
corners of her mouth, and very, very still.

As for being PATIENT, Alison sighed and blended
the lot—the blinking with the lip biting and the lip
biting with the faint smile and the slightly uptilted
chin (a very difficult feat)—and then, keeping it all nice
and steady and fixed, she turned back to the window,
there to test herself by conjuring all the pleasures and
promises and beauties outside, so that she would then be
able to fight back the temptation to groan at her awful
bad luck.

And indeed it was a pleasurable, promising, and beautiful view she looked out upon from the third-floor window
of that rambling old house which the McNairs had
rented for the summer. Even through the fly screen,
everything looked so clear and clean under the cloudless
sky that it was hard to imagine that New York was only
an hour-or-so's drive away, or that the temperature out
there must be in the upper eighties. Every tree and bush
on the hillside looming opposite could have been made

out clearly by anyone who really had the time and the curiosity to identify them—yet they must have been between one and two miles away. Alison thought of the trails winding in and out and around, under those trees, and of the pony she could have been riding along them, if only she'd been able to go out and enjoy herself. (And had been able to rent or borrow a pony, and had been able to ride it properly when she'd acquired it.)

"Alison . . . ?"

Jeannie's voice had a lonely, plaintive note in it.

Alison fought down her natural scorn and remembered she was being PATIENT.

"Yes?"

"What are you doing?"

"Nothing *you* need worry about . . . honey."

"No, but *what?*"

Jeannie's new note of irritation pleased Alison. It set off her own feeling of PATIENCE—long-suffering, good, calm PATIENCE—very nicely.

"Just looking out of the window, dear."

"What at?"

"The view, that's all."

"Oh . . ."

Jeannie sounded satisfied. Jeannie was so easily satisfied. Alison felt glad that she herself would ever be one of the restless ones, the searchers, the experimenters, the explorers—the salt of the earth.

Then she went back to being PATIENT.

Between the grounds of the house and the hillside, there was rough pasture, spattered with tall, coarse yellow flowers which Alison would dearly have loved to feel brushing against her naked legs as she made her way to the lake, over to the right, a blue finger of which came curling around between the spurs in a break in the hills. She could see a white sail, drifting under a sandy bluff at the water's edge. Maybe it was the boat her brother, Tom, had borrowed—lucky dog. *He'd* had the measles fifteen years ago, when he was only two, an age when it didn't matter so much whether you had to stay indoors or not. Why, oh why, couldn't *she* have had them at that age? Or at least during the winter, during schooltime, or—

"PATIENCE!" whispered an inner voice—and Alison quickly smoothed out her brow and lifted her chin and closed her mouth and smiled her faint perfectly balanced smile.

Even so, it was touch and go whether she could maintain that pose, until she forced herself to look away from the lake and gaze steadily down at the garden instead.

She sighed gently again.

"Alison . . ."

"Yes, honey?"

"You still looking at the view?"

"Yes, honey."

"Are there some boys out there?"

"No."

Alison's carefully preserved expression wavered a little here. No doubt there *would* be boys out there somewhere. Out by the lake there must have been. Tom's friends. Other boys. Splashing and sailing and fooling around. Brown bodies diving, swimming underwater, and coming up behind, grabbing your ankle and—

"Who *is* out there then?"

"Come and—"

Alison caught back the words like a boy grabbing at an ankle.

But it was all right. Jeannie had heard, but she had no intention of joining her and breaking the spell.

"I can't. Mom said I'd have to stay in here another day, away from the bright light. You shouldn't be looking out into the sun, either."

"I thought you wanted to know who was out there."

"Oh . . . yes . . . Who?"

"Just Mom, practicing her putting on the lawn just underneath. And someone farther down, in the vegetable part behind the currant bushes."

"Who?"

Here Alison was sorely tempted to say: "A wild-looking man with a beard and an ax in his hand, creeping up on Mom"—just to liven up the afternoon and have Jeannie scampering and screaming to her side. But she was being PATIENT, she reminded herself.

"Just the gardener," she said. "That Mr. Whatsisname."

"Crowther."

Jeannie was good at names.

"Yes, he looks it."

"Looks what?"

"Like a Groucher."

"I said Crowther."

"I know you did."

Alison sighed again as she looked down at the tall, thin man in the red and black checkered shirt, stooping over the cabbage patch or whatever it was that he was

weeding. He had a bald yellow head and sticking-out ears, and although he couldn't help that side of his looks, he surely could have done something about his expression, which was sour and all pursed up, and became even sourer and pursier whenever he looked around toward the house. Alison had heard her mother laugh about the gardener, saying to Mr. McNair one evening at the beginning: "I'm sure he hates people staying here, even though it's visitors like us who keep him in his job."

Alison could well believe this as she studied his expression just then. That was why she sighed. To a healthy active girl like her the grouches of this world are fair game, and she was thinking of all the sport she could have had with this one if she'd been fully mobile.

"PATIENCE," commended the inner voice again.

But what with the weather and the woods and the lake and the thoughts of ponies and boys and a real live worthy enemy on the premises, Alison's PATIENT pose was beginning to crack and chip at the edges. There was an antidote to this, however—one that had come to her rescue several times in the past—and she took it before her act could be broken up beyond repair. She switched to a similar type of mood, but one that was much easier to maintain, and the name of it was WISTFUL.

She worked at it, keeping her PATIENT expression basically, but raising her eyebrows a little, just above her nose, and—very slowly, very gently, so that the movement was hardly perceptible—shaking her head from side to side.

She might just as well have been back in New York, she told herself. Really she might. If her only contact with the outside world was looking out of a window, she might as well be doing it back home.

WISTFULLY—oh, so very WISTFULLY—she thought about the view from her room on the fifth story of the old brownstone on East Seventy-fifth Street. Since it was a back room, the view wasn't a very busy one—just the backs of the buildings in the next street. But there was always something happening, either at the windows or in the yards down below. True, there wasn't much in the way of greenery: a few small mountain ashes and a ragged cherry by the fence that ran between their place and the high new apartment building directly opposite; and three or four tall, thin ginkgoes in a line at right angles, alongside the fence that divided the big new building from its neighbor, an old, decayed, crumbly gray house—older and crumblier even than this one out in the country. But who wanted greenery when one was stuck indoors, a prisoner, like this?

"Alison . . . ?"

Back on Seventy-fifth Street, even if it was the summer vacation, having measles wouldn't have been half so bad. She would have had so many interesting people to watch and wonder about and maybe wave to. Maids in their white uniforms over in the new building, cooking in the kitchens or watering plants along the windowsills, under the venetian blinds. The fat man just opposite but a little lower, doing his chest exercises with the window open and cheating (every time you saw him he cheated). The two little boys with their solemn shiny faces, working at their home assignments every afternoon, with the globe of the world making it *three* round solemn faces—never smiling, never fooling around, never cheating, just drawing or writing or reading away until a dark-haired woman with tight lips, some sort of tutor, came and sat between them and went through what they had done, still unsmiling. Confined to her own window with measles, what a great opportunity it would have been for Alison, what a wonderful game, to give some time and thought to catching their attention and holding it and doing things—faces and things—to make them laugh and *then* see what happened.

"*Alison!*"

"Huh? . . . What?"

"What are you doing now?"

"I'm looking out of the window."

"There *are* some boys there, aren't there?"

"Yes—those two—" Alison sighed deeply. "I mean no. No. There aren't any boys. Just Mom still. And the Groucher."

"You said two boys, I heard you."

"Yes, well, that was another window."

"What other window? There's only one in there."

"Another window far away. Back home. I—I was in a trance. I—my spirit—oh, you wouldn't understand!"

"Yes I would, yes I would! Tell me!"

Alison turned angrily. But then she had an idea, and smiled.

"My spirit had flown out of my body. My body stayed here, but my spirit went floating, floating away, all the way back home, and was looking out of the window there."

"What did it see then?"

"Those two boys opposite—those who're always doing their homework at the window."

"What were they doing?"

"Their homework, of course."

"I don't believe you."

"Only this time something sinister was lurking in back of them. Some—some kind of shadow."

"What? What was it?"

"You wouldn't believe me."

"I would, I would! Please tell me what it was."

"I don't know myself. You woke me out of my trance before I could make it out."

"Well—well, go back into it again. Will you, Alison? Please?"

"Oh, all right! I'll try. But you'll have to be very quiet. You won't say a word. Promise?"

"Yes, yes. I promise."

"O.K., then . . ."

So Alison won some more peace for being WISTFUL in, but it wasn't the same. Try as she might, she couldn't see the view from the Seventy-fifth Street window anything like as clearly as before. She tried to concentrate on the old gray building with the little yard in front of the second-floor bay window, where an old woman lived —a little square yard that was raised up from the basement area on a kind of brick pedestal, like one of those platforms in the front of old ships—fo'c'sles, she thought they called them. . . .

But the yard with its dirty old round iron table and iron chairs, where the white-haired lady of the apartment sometimes used to sit polishing spoons or brushing her cat—no, it wouldn't come at all clearly. All she could see instead was the large smooth smiling face of her best friend Emmeline, turning to her and saying:

"*I* think she's an old hermit, who used to be very beautiful and who was madly in love with a young man who got himself killed in a fight in her honor, the night before they were due to be married. . . ."

Alison smiled, really wistfully now, not even conscious of it.

For if only Emmeline had been out here in the country with them, how different it would have been, what fun they would have had, measles or no measles! Why, there'd even been a chance that Emmeline might come with them. "Mother and Father say it's O.K. by them, Alison, so long as yours don't mind."

But no.

Mrs. McNair didn't approve of Emmeline.

"Emmeline is always leading you into mischief," she had said. "It's bad enough that you see her so much every day, here in New York. But all day and all night, every day and every night, for six or seven weeks—no."

And that was rotten unfair, Alison thought angrily now. Really and truly and—and *despicably* unfair. Because the truth was that Emmeline *never* led her into mischief, never had done, never would. All her mother was going by was the fact that sometimes Alison had blamed Emmeline, made an excuse saying it had been Emmeline's idea, just to put an end to the nag-nag-nagging. Emmeline didn't mind. But that was no reason *really* to hold it against the girl. Mrs. McNair ought to have realized that. A good mother ought to be able to judge these things better and to know whether her own daughter could really be led into mischief by someone as sweet and innocent and docile as Emmeline.

"Yergh! Miss it!" she hissed softly through the fly screen, as she bent to watch her mother getting ready to putt the golf ball.

It was an easy shot. The ball was only about five inches from the plastic cup. But just as if the draft from Alison's hiss had carried all that distance down to the lawn, gathering strength on its way, the ball curved gently but determinedly away from the cup.

Mrs. McNair made a little cluck of annoyance mixed with amazement. She straightened up, her figure slight and boyish in shirt and slacks, and cleared a stray wisp of her thin sandy hair away from her forehead, the way she did when she was baffled or vexed.

Alison blinked, somewhat surprised herself. Then she drew back from the window, feeling almost as if she had really been responsible for the miss, and not wanting her mother to glance up and see her there.

The sudden movement must have been heard in the next room.

"Alison—oh, sorry!"

"Hmmm?"

"I'm sorry. Did I get you out of your trance?"

Alison frowned, then grinned secretly.

"Yes, you did!"

"Sorry, Alison. What are you doing now?"

"Reading."

"Reading?"

"Yes . . ."

Alison had crossed to a low bookshelf at the side of the old black sofa and was running a finger along the backs of the top row.

"What about your eyes?"

"Oh, be quiet! I'm only reading the titles."

And that is all she might have done, for they weren't very inspiring titles (like *The Collected Sermons of a New England Parish Priest*, *A Handbook of Greek Mythology*, *The History of Pound Ridge*, and *Notes on Isometrization Reactions of Organic Compounds*). But then something happened. Toward the end of the row, her finger slipped into the niche made by a book that had been pushed farther back than the rest.

"Ouch!" she gasped as she felt her nail being clutched by something sharp and ridgy, with something else pricking the tip of her finger. "You—you *witch!*"

Why she should have used that particular word, she never did find out. It wasn't one of her favorite swear words, after all, although she had been known to fall back on it occasionally when she hadn't dared to use anything stronger.

But this time it had come out fast, without her having to do any thinking, and it was therefore no wonder that she gasped again and gaped when, opening the greasy dog-eared gray-black cover (for the spine had been ripped off, or clawed off, or chewed off, long since, leaving only the bare spiky ridges of hard glue that had stabbed her finger), she saw the title:

The Secret Arts of Witchcraft and How to Become an Adept

CHAPTER 3

Ariadne M. . . .

Alison would never forget that moment, in the old attic room with the shabby furniture, the pictures made of pressed dried flowers, the tarnished mirror in the heavy gilt frame, the sofa of a curious black, as if its cover had been soaked in tar and allowed to gather dust before it dried, and the bookcase, chipped and scratched, filled with what looked like volumes that had been bought at a garage sale in dusty bundles tied with hairy string. Never would she forget the musty smell that rose from the pages of the witchcraft book as she turned them, or the faint crackle of the dried glue along the spine as it reacted to her eager handling.

The paper was smooth, quite thin, but yellowed, particularly at the edges. Every page she turned to seemed to have been well thumbed, pondered over, dwelt upon. Apart from certain greasy thumbprints, there were other signs of this heavy usage. Words had been underlined, some in uneven indelible pencil, with violet smudges here and there like blood blisters, and some in ink—mainly a blue-black fading to brown, but occasionally a fresher bolder green.

And some of the pages were stained.

Especially were they stained in the section headed (in the rather old-fashioned curly-looking print) "Ingredients for Spells." There were deep yellow splashes of what looked like sulfur but could have been dried milk. There were brown rings, as of rust from the bottoms of rough iron cups or bowls. There was one smear of what might very well have been blood, and there was another of what certainly *was* blood (for the withered body of the crushed fly was still adhering to it).

Slowly, carefully, Alison examined the book, page by page, looking for marks rather than words, treating it not so much as a book as an object—a kind of strange purse with many pockets, pouches, secret cavities. And as she searched, she began to grip it less firmly, and eventually she found herself holding it lightly, with the flat of her left hand, the fingers stiff, ready to drop it if something unexpected should dart out.

Then, reaching the end and noting that several pages had been torn out, leaving only the beginning of the final chapter ("A Serious Warning to Those Who Would Dabble"), she turned back to the flyleaves to see if anything had been written there by one of the original owners.

And yes—she tilted the book toward the light—there were two inscriptions. There was a name, or the beginning of a name, in the faded brownish ink: *Frede.* . . . The rest had been rubbed out, hurriedly but also viciously, it seemed, making a dark smudge and a small hole in the paper. Then, over the top of it, in the green ink, bold and flourishing like a sapling springing from a rotted stump, was another name, *Ariadne,* followed by the initial letter *M.*

Alison felt a curious prickling sensation at the back of her neck as she thought about those names. That is to say, she *made* herself feel a curious prickling sensation, which was one of her acts, coming under the general heading SINISTER, or STUMBLING OVER SOMETHING SINISTER. But this time the prickling came through stronger than it had ever done before, and it didn't need any working on to keep it going. For it really did seem that what she was gazing on was the record of the result of an old battle, a battle of witches, between the older, feebler *Frede* . . . and the vigorous, flourishing *Ariadne M.*

Alison wondered about *Frede.* . . . Maybe it had
been the name of a boy—no, a man, an old ugly grouch-
type man, a wizard, *Frederick*, and if so it served him
right for dabbling in a female art. But more likely it
was a woman's name, *Frederica* maybe—a woman who'd
grown old and careless, thoughtless of anyone except
herself, in which case it served *her* right, also. In fact,
man or woman, grouch or simply thoughtless, he or she
deserved to be vanquished by someone as young and
vigorous as Ariadne M. Why, she had the same initials as Alison herself!

This set the prickling going stronger than ever. But
now it was a joyful promising prickling that came creeping around her neck and up under her ears and across
her cheeks like the measles themselves. Of course! The
book was meant for *her*, Alison McNair. It had been left
there purposely, placed and preserved under a spell that
had kept other eyes from seeing it and other probing
fingers at bay for—oh, who knew *how* long? A whole
chain of events had been carefully prepared to lead her
to it, that was certain. I mean, she told herself, would
she ever have even glanced at those books, weather like
this, if she hadn't been confined in there with the
measles? Hurrah for the measles! They'd been part of it.

And hadn't there—now she came to think of it—been
something spooky about that afternoon? Not the fooling
with the doll and its vampire teeth—that wasn't spooky,
that was just sport. But afterward, in here, at the
window. The clearness and stillness of everything. The
talk of being in a trance. Well, maybe she *had* been in a
trance at that. Maybe her spirit *had* been traveling back

home, without her body, way up over Bedford and White Plains, Mount Vernon and the Bronx, and down, looping over the Triboro Bridge, into their apartment on Seventy-fifth Street. After all, it *had* been a very clear picture of the view from her window. . . . *Crystal* clear. . . . And what about the strange behavior of the golf ball?

The Secret Arts of Witchcraft and How to Become an Adept . . .

She read the title over carefully, thoughtfully, nodding slowly as she did so.

Yes, there could be no doubt about it.

She, Alison McNair, was destined to become a witch, just as Ariadne M. obviously had become one, after reading this very book.

She turned to the first chapter, headed "Preliminary Steps." She didn't intend to give it more than a glance-over before concentrating on the Spells, for, having shown such strong signs of witchcraft earlier, Alison felt that she was a natural and could therefore safely skip most of the fundamentals. But then she remembered reading somewhere that it didn't do to be too smart in the early stages of a witch's apprenticeship, so she put on her HUMBLE face (chin dipped into chest, eyes narrower than usual, with a doubled blink-rate) and began to read Chapter 1 with all due care.

Approach with respect or close this book forever. . . .

These were the very first words, and they seemed to match so well the thoughts she'd been thinking that she couldn't help feeling that she was being watched, her every move and thought monitored by some spirit supervisor. So she decided she'd better be HUMBLE in spades and go back a few pages and read the Introduction as well—something she'd never deigned to do in her life before.

Maybe it was as well that she did, too. In the very first paragraph of the Introduction, she came across these words:

> *Far from having to be raven-haired, a witch can have any coloring. Indeed, the most powerful witches of all—regarded in awe and feared by the knowledgeable from time immemorial—have been those with red hair.*

Alison just couldn't help it. Her heart gave such a leap at this that she had to do something.

"Yowee!" she yelled. And: "Just imagine!"

There came a light thump from the other room, and a padding of feet.

"What? What have you seen?"

Jeannie was at the door.

Alison closed the book and tried to look nonchalant. "Nothing . . . Only my thoughts."

"Was it something in that book?"

"I told you." Alison moved over to the window seat with the book in her hand. "It was just something I thought."

Jeannie blinked against the stronger light.

"Was it something dirty? Is it a dirty book?"

"This?" Alison laughed scornfully. "Nergh! It's just some old book about witches. . . . Hey, look at you! You shouldn't be straining your eyes in this light."

"Will you tell me a story about witches, Alison?"

"O.K. Sure. Later. Go back to bed and I'll tell you a witch story later."

"In the dark? Tonight?"

"In the dark. Tonight."

"Oh, goody!"

"Yes. Now back to bed and I'll try to find something really juicy for you."

Powerfully, Alison smiled as she settled down powerfully to read. Powerful Alison M., the red-haired witch (she was powerfully thinking), might very well have something much better than a story for her little sister, come the night and darkness. Something properly, fittingly powerful; some actual act; some specimen spell . . .

CHAPTER 4

The Gesture of Defiance

"Alison . . ."

The whisper came stabbing across in the darkness, piercing the other night noises—the chirping of crickets, the hum of the air conditioner, the faint drone of voices coming from somewhere below.

Alison held herself still. She was tired. She wanted to go to sleep. Preparing to be a witch was turning out to be much harder work than she'd imagined, and there was still a lot to be done in the morning. She yawned softly—but not softly enough.

"You're awake, Alison, I know you are! I heard you yawn, and nobody ever yawns in their sleep—you told me that yourself once."

"What? What is it you want?"

"You know what. You promised me. You promised me this afternoon."

"Huh! You mean a spell? O.K., then. Vanish!"

"Spell? What do you mean? You promised me a story. A witch story."

Alison sighed, rolling her eyes in the darkness. Sure as anything, as soon as she learned the skills, she'd do

something about that sister of hers. Nothing dreadful.
Nothing final. Just something to fix that tongue of hers
at times when you wanted to think or read or sleep.

"Alison . . ."

"Oh, all right! I—" Alison clasped her hands behind
her neck and wriggled into a more comfortable position
while she thought about what she was going to say.
Then it came: "I'll tell you about a Beginner Witch,
O.K.?"

"A Beginner Witch?"

"Yes. A beautiful girl who decided to be a witch,
and—"

"What was her name?"

"Oh—*Ariadne*. Yes. *Ariadne*."

"Sounds like a good witch name. Go on."

"The best, honey. I looked—I mean, *she* looked it up
in an old book about the Greek gods and goddesses, and
Ariadne was the daughter of a king, the one who owned
a maze with a bull monster in it, and she helped
people to escape and—"

"I don't want to hear about monsters; I want to hear
about this girl witch. Was that her real name?"

"No, it was her *witch* name, one of them. When you
become a witch you have to pick a new name. Some
who're going to be very powerful witches pick two. And
some who're going to be the most powerful of all, they
pick *three* witch names."

"Oh. . . ." Jeannie sounded as if she were losing
interest. Alison was relieved. She'd just been on the
brink of disclosing her own particular choice of *Ariadne*

Atropos Arachne (all from the *Handbook of Greek Mythology*, which seemed to have been put on the bookshelf for a useful purpose after all). She remembered the Great Rule of Secrecy and told herself to be careful.

"What was her real name?"

Alison started at the crisp suddenness of the question.

"Er—I—I'm not sure I know," she said, still urging herself to be careful. "Anyway, it doesn't matter. Ariadne was her chief name as a witch. She—"

"What did she look like?"

"Oh . . ." Alison sighed and settled herself again, closing her eyes. "Beautiful," she murmured, "really beautiful. She had red hair, beautiful red hair—"

"Like me! Oh, good! I mean, she *was* a good witch, wasn't she, Alison?"

"One of the very best," said Alison tartly. "How could she be anything else if she looked even a little like you?"

"I like this story. Go on."

"Yes, well. Don't expect any miracles yet. This is only the story of how she started learning to be a witch and—oh . . ." She yawned. "Sorry! Learning to be a witch isn't all that easy."

"Finding a name's easy. I think I'd pick Ariadne, too. Go on."

"No you wouldn't!" Alison was up on one elbow now, scowling through the darkness. "You wouldn't if she'd picked it first. Or—or you'd be punished."

"Pu-punished?"

"Yes. That's a terrible thing. Picking the name another

witch has already picked, just because she picked it. I suppose if I'd chosen—I mean *she'd* chosen *Sylvie* or—or *Vampira*—you'd have chosen that one."

"But—it's only a story, Alison. Isn't it?"

Alison frowned, then slowly shook her head. There hadn't been the least trace of sarcasm in her sister's voice as far as she could detect. The kid was just dumb, that was all.

"Sure," she said, more sweetly, "sure. It's just that I got carried away for a while. I can see it all so vividly, you see." She closed her eyes in the darkness, feeling a tingle of cunning run through the roots of her lashes. "Just as if it had happened to me."

"Well, you've got reddish hair too, Alison," said Jeannie, in a maddeningly consoling sort of voice.

"Hmm . . . yes . . . Anyway, about Ariadne. After picking a name for herself, her next big task was to make a Gesture."

"What's that? Something like an altar in church?"

"No, no! Though come to think of it, that does come on the list later," Alison added thoughtfully, feeling rather weary again. Then she brightened. She was rather proud of her own particular Gesture and wanted to communicate something of this feeling. "No, a gesture is, well, something you *do*. Something you do to show something, to prove something. Like a token, a—a gesture. Right?"

"Oh, yes," came Jeannie's still somewhat uncertain voice. "Yes. Sure. A gesture."

"And this gesture—the Witch's Gesture—has to be a Gesture of Defiance. Something to do with old rules—to

show you're breaking away from them and don't care.
Right? See what I mean?"

"Yes—I think so."

"Well, what the Witch books usually tell you to do is
say the Lord's Prayer backwards every night for three
nights."

"Oh, no!" gasped Jeannie.

"Oh, yes!" said Alison grimly. "But don't worry. I—
I mean Ariadne—she didn't like the sound of that any
more than you do. I mean three nights is all right for
ordinary Beginner Witches. But not those with red hair,
who're so much more powerful anyway."

"Yes, but—"

"I know, I know! And red-haired Beginner Witches
who're going to put all their extra power into being
good witches don't go messing about with the Lord's
Prayer, or even the Ten Commandments—though Ariadne
did think about *them* for a time."

"What then? What rules and things did *she* say backwards?"

"Why"—here Alison sat straight up in bed, she felt so
proud—"the rules that bugged her most. Those she really
would have to free herself from if she was ever going to
concentrate on being a witch. Like—you want to hear
them?"

"Yes, please, Alison."

"Be quiet then, and listen. I'll say them backwards,
the way she did—the top ten commandments in *her*
house—and you see if you can guess them. Ready?"

"Right!"

"Number One: *Tairts pu tis.*"

"What?"

"*Tairts pu tis.*"

"Er—can you say it again, Alison? I didn't quite—"

"Oh, never mind! We'll be all night at this rate. I'll give you them the right way around, the Ten Rules that Ali—er—Ariadne said backwards:

"One: *Sit up straight.*"

"Why?"

"That's the *rule*, stupid! The one I said backwards for you. The one they—her parents—were forever yacking at her."

"Oh, yes! Like—"

"Two: *Don't speak to your mother like that.*"

"Tath kile—"

"Three: *Ask before you leave the table.*"

"That's what—"

"Four: *Try to have some consideration for others.*"

"Ooh, that would be hard to say backwards! Con—consideration."

"Takes you all your time to say it forwards. Five: *Go and brush your teeth.*"

"I did already—oh, yes—you mean—"

"Six: *Eating in bedrooms is forbidden.* Seven: *Turn that thing down.* (You know, like when we're listening to some *real* music.) Eight: *He's far too old for you.*"

"Who? Who's too old?"

"Anybody. Any boy Ariadne happens to like, just like, nothing more."

"You're saying all the things Mom says to us. And sometimes Daddy says."

"Sure. Ariadne was a girl, remember. Like us. An

ordinary American girl, tied hand and foot—a slave. Tied
hand and foot by ordinary American family rules. You
want to finish this yourself?"

"No. Go on. Eight—or Nine, was it?"

"Nine: *Save up for it the way we had to do at your
age.* And Ten: *Be quiet and go to sleep.*"

"That's *just* like *our* rules!" cried Jeannie.

"Yes, well—"

Alison broke off at the sound of her father's voice
from the door of the sitting room.

"You hear me? It's after eleven already. *Be quiet and
go to sleep!*"

This was too much. Both girls dug their faces into
their pillows, gasping silently, almost hysterical, kicking
their mattresses in an effort to stifle the hoots of laughter
that wanted to come shooting out.

And by the time they had conquered the fit they
were too exhausted to go on with the story.

"I—I'll tell you more tomorrow," murmured Alison.
"About—oh, about all the things she had to collect—
her equipment—the Necklace—the Garter—they all have
to have a garter, most important. . . . And the tools,
the Witch's Tools, like a cup, a special cup, and a knife
with a black handle, and special cord with special knots
for a Girdle, and a Workbook. . . . Oh, and charcoal
blocks and—and candles—and salt, lots of salt. . . . And
a pen—only it has to be a dip pen—and ink, black ink,
though I think green might be better—and lots of jars
and bottles—for potions and things, you know. . . . And
a table, a kind of altar and workbench combined. . . .
And—did I say salt?—lots of salt—yes—and a den of

course, a secret, private place, a special out-of-the-way room—and I think I know just the place—I mean Ariadne —*she* thought she knew just the place. . . ."

But Alison/Ariadne needn't have worried about that last slip. Jeannie was already fast asleep, her breathing deep and regular, just as . . . just as . . . just as . . .

So, deep into the oldest, strongest spell of all fell the fledgling Ariadne Atropos Arachne herself—keeper and cutter and spinner of threads all in one, according to the Handbook. . . .

CHAPTER 5

A Witch's Treasure House

Rarely, if ever, can a witch have started up in business so hastily and haphazardly equipped as Alison McNair. And the reasons for this were threefold.

To begin with, there was the natural impatience and impetuousness of the witch-to-be in question: a girl who could never wait contentedly for paint to dry, or water to boil, or cakes to rise, or frost to thaw, or seeds to shoot, or savings to grow, or spots to vanish of their own accord. Furthermore, she was the sort of girl whom even the adults most closely connected with her training soon grew to despair of, recognizing that such impetuousness was elemental, incurable, monumental, and that she was destined to go through life like that, becoming a woman who couldn't wait for lights to turn green, or plots to hatch, or the people around her to make up their minds.

Secondly—to be fair—there was the reason that could have affected any learner witch, no matter how patient she might happen to be: the restrictions imposed by being an invalid—confined to the house—and a strange house at that. Had Alison been back home during these

early days, knowing just what the apartment contained
and where every article was to be found, she would have
embarked on her new career in a much better state of
readiness.

But thirdly—and most importantly—there was her confidence, her supreme sense of confidence in everything
she undertook. Some used to call this arrogance, and
talk about fools rushing in where angels feared to tread.
Others weren't so sure. For it was the sort of spirit
that gets things done, even if they don't turn out to
be done precisely in the way originally envisaged, or
even required; while others, of a more careful and less
confident kind, go on pussyfooting around a project
forever, until they get tired of it, and drop it, and turn
their timid, cautious attention to something new. What's
more, this sense of supreme confidence wasn't to be
confused with Alison's basic impatience. It wasn't an
excuse for rushing on regardless. Even if she had been at
home and various prescribed things had been available
(like the Necklace, to name just one), the chances are
that in her confidence she would have decided to reject
some of them, feeling convinced she had a better idea.

Anyone who'd been privileged to see her poring over
that book in the early stages, checking on the basic
equipment required, would soon have come to understand this most vividly. For Alison was a talkative reader,
as might be expected with someone of her imaginative,
impetuous nature. That is to say, she didn't merely
mumble under her breath the words she happened to be
reading. She commented upon them, often quite forcibly,
and even made direct remarks to the writer of the book,

like: "Way to go, ma'am!" or "Come *on!*" or "You don't
say!" And in this case, so caught up was she in the
subject, so intensely concerned was she, that she expanded
her shadowy audience, taking in not only the author of
the book but also the bold Ariadne M., who'd been
there before, and the feeble Frede . . . , for whom she'd
conceived a mild dislike, or contempt, for being (she
felt sure) one of the humble pussyfooters of this world.

So, if the author should propose something that
looked impossible—like requiring the reader to purchase
some out-of-the-way herb like hellebore root, which Alison
felt sure she'd have difficulty in getting even in New
York, even at the A&P—she'd turn to the flyleaf and,
addressing the firm green flourish of *Ariadne M.*, say:

"Who's she think she's kidding—*hellebore* root?"

And, in her mind's ear, the soul of Ariadne M. would
respond with:

"Forget it, Alison. Use what your instinct tells you is
best. *You're* a natural, and this is just for plodders."

Then sometimes—though less and less frequently—the
faded, frightened Frede . . . would try to remonstrate,
saying, in a kind of frayed whisper:

"Oh, but you must do exactly what the writer tells you
to—"

Whereupon both Alison and the soul of Ariadne M.
would turn on the fink and say: "Aw, be quiet!" or
"Much good it did *you!*" or simply "Shaddap!"

Somehow this boldness, this confidence, seemed to
win the approval of the writer herself. Again and again,
after these shadowy debates, Alison would turn back to
the passage that had started it all and discover, by re-

reading it or the lines just before or just after it, that it wasn't indeed compulsory to get such and such a particular herb after all, or to say certain things in a certain special order, or wear a particular article. Substitutes could be used—and a free choice of them made—or they could be left out altogether—"*so long as the feeling is powerful enough and vivid enough.*"

Those were the author's favorite words; and they soon came to be Alison's too, just as they'd obviously been Ariadne M.'s.

So some of the items she'd listed in her bedtime talk with Jeannie that first night were skipped—either with or without the author's open blessing. Of the Witch's Jewels, for example, all had been declared "optional" save the Necklace. Out therefore went the Bracelet, the Ring, and the Pendant (with the possibility of getting them later if she wanted, on her return to New York), while the Girdle Cord and the Garter were retained chiefly because the idea of them took her fancy and she thought she could see her way to making them out of material she could find in the house.

Of the Witch's Tools, the White-hilted Knife was the first to be crossed off, but for another reason. True, the author had been a bit vague as to whether it was compulsory or not, but what really decided its fate with Alison was the description of its purpose: "*for engraving the smaller details on other items of equipment, etc.*" This, to her mind, smacked too much of the fussing that went on in school: marking your books and putting name tags on clothes—activities she loathed for being passive, unproductive, getting nowhere very slowly. Fiddling about with engraving might be all right for feeble souls like Frede . . . (though much good it had done *her* in the end), but the only markings Alison meant to make were big ones, bold ones, deeply scored but rapidly executed ones, in black earth on black midnights, and for that there would be the great Black-handled Knife, or, as it was called, the Athamé. (Which, being yet another A, just had to be important and could not, under any circumstances, be left out.)

Finally (dealing with the items she rejected), there was the question of the Ink of Art and the Pen of Art.

The writer of the book had been very specific here, saying the ink *"should be black, of the kind used for maps and posters,"* and recommending that the beginner make her own from a given recipe. And on the subject of pens she had said straight out: *"This must be a dip pen, NOT a ball-point."*

What helped Alison to decide was partly the recipe (where on earth could she get powdered peach kernel at such short notice?) and partly the tone. No doubt the author of the book had been a successful witch herself, but there were places where it became all too clear that in public life she'd been a teacher with strict old-fashioned tastes, like Miss Timmins, the art teacher at Alison's school—and this was one of them. Miss Timmins had views on ball-points too, and her reaction to the use of any ink other than black for special work had only last semester reduced Alison's best friend Emmeline to tears.

So Alison, with another glance at the bold flourish of *Ariadne M.* and a sneer for the obedient but faded black

Frede . . . , sidled into the downstairs sitting room
when no one was around and took from the bureau
drawer that housed her parents' writing materials the
green ball-point pen that she'd known to be there and
had had her heart set on ever since seeing her predecessor's scrawls in the book.

Apart from these exceptions, she did quite dutifully
and humbly stick to the prescribed list, even though
some of the articles taxed her ingenuity and others put
her to considerable risk.

On the whole, the simplest were the kitchen things—
or, rather, those that could be found in the kitchen even
if the witch uses they were destined for were far removed
from cooking or eating or drinking. And here Alison
was very lucky, for the kitchen of that house, having
passed through many generations of vacationers and
visitors, had accumulated all manner of odds and ends of
utensils and gadgets until it had grown to be a cross
between a folklore museum, a pawn shop, a junk yard,
and an Aladdin's Cave.

The fact that it was huge—a great rambling country
kitchen with strange angles and several off-shooting store-
rooms, washrooms, and closets—had not retarded this
process. Every cupboard was crammed, and likely to burst
open with a resounding rattle and clank; half the drawers
were jammed shut, they were so full; and there wasn't a
single shelf out of a total of over fifty that had space
left for so much as one extra good-sized pack of cereal.
Mrs. McNair had been grumbling about it ever since
she'd arrived, threatening daily to have a grand clear-up—
and probably she would have done something about it,

too, if Alison and Jeannie had been up and well enough
to do all the tedious work. As it was, however, it was a
treasure house, a Witch's Treasure House, with everything so hopelessly jumbled that it would take weeks for
an article to be missed. If ever.

So Alison was able to get, in a mere half-hour during
the morning, while her mother was out shopping and
the lower floors were deserted:

> enough salt to exorcise an army of evil spirits
> ("ground rock salt" at that, just what the book
> had recommended as the best);

> half a sack of charcoal blocks of the self-ignit-
> ing type;

> a dozen unused white candles;

> a dozen assorted jars and small bottles, empty
> but clean, and all with screw caps;

> a chafing dish, electric, which she prized above
> all her other kitchen booty;

> a large chunky glass goblet, which she only
> wished had been made of metal, but which in
> shape was just right; and

> exactly the right kind of knife: sharp-pointed,
> steel (its tarnishing showed that), about 6 in.
> long in the blade; and with a handle that might
> possibly have started out as a dark brown wood
> but was now as black as could make no
> difference.

There were also a number of other things she took

from the kitchen, things that had not been on her original list. But more about them later.

Among the items on her list that gave her a certain amount of trouble mentally—in figuring out ways to improvise them—the Workbook, the Garter, and the Necklace were prominent.

The Workbook, as the repository of all the witch's secrets—her accounts of progress, her recipes, her spells, her incantations—had to be something special, even Alison had to agree. Naturally, all the fussy Miss Timmins-like art-teacherishness came out in the writer of the book at this point, with talk of buying expensive parchment, and making careful measurements, and sewing it up yourself, and covering it with a special material. Yet even though she rebelled against this, Alison couldn't bring herself simply to snatch up a note pad from the downstairs desk and make that do. For one thing, it was a Peanuts Pad, with a little picture of Charlie Brown in the top corner of every page, and somehow that didn't seem to go with witchcraft at all. Then again, it wasn't really big enough for all the spells that Ariadne Atropos Arachne was going to cast, let alone for the potions she proposed to brew and the incantations she meant to compose and chant.

The Garter posed a similar problem. Oh, sure—she could have used one of her own or Jeannie's velvet hair bands, tightening the elastic to make it small enough to hold firm on the leg in the prescribed place (just above the left knee). After all, it wasn't as if the writer of the book left her with no choice of color. Black would have done, or green, both of which were available as hair bands. But *"the traditional color is red, bright blood red,"* the writer had added—and for some reason nothing other than a bright red garter would have satisfied Alison. What was more, she had an overwhelming yen for something else the writer had mentioned—this time as the merest optional trimming: *"a little gold or silver bell stitched onto the Garter."* So something red it had to be—with bells on.

"But *why?*" the shade of Ariadne M. had seemed to say, when Alison turned to the flyleaf to test her feelings on this. "Why make extra work for yourself?"

"Yes," she thought she heard Frede . . . croak, for once in agreement, "even I would not—"

"That's why!" said Alison then, quite loud, snapping the book shut, firmly convinced now that that was the sort of Garter she should have.

As for the Necklace, here again she needn't have been stuck for a single moment. Her mother had a drawerful of beads of one kind or another—many of them of the wooden Indian chunky kind recommended by the writer of the book. Mrs. McNair would never have missed just one string of them—or if she had she'd only have thought she'd left them back in New York. But *borrowed* beads, for that most important of all the Witch's Jewels, seemed so enfeebling—something that could throw everything wrong, right from the start. And beads borrowed from one's *mother* . . .

Alison shook her head so vigorously at the very thought of such a thing that it was a wonder sparks didn't fly from her hair.

And even when she'd solved the Workbook problem

(by annexing an old little-used telephone numbers book she found downstairs, with a very special-looking soft brown leather cover with a pattern of red diamonds and golden circles on it, and only a few of the pages needing to be torn out), and had woven herself a Garter from a number of rubber bands of a bright enough red (snapping and retying them and running them through the handle of a small brass servants' bell from the dining-room sideboard cupboard), she didn't weaken in regard to the Necklace.

"If I can solve the first two, I can solve *that!*" she told herself fiercely.

And solve it she did—but only in the third phase of her searchings: the one in which she took such great risks. . . .

CHAPTER 6

Problems and Perils—
with Graywing and Browntail

The author of *The Secret Arts of Witchcraft and How to Become an Adept* had been very clear about the table and the Girdle. Regarding the first, she had written:

> Your Worktable, or "Altar," or "Table of Practice," must be square—ideally about 2 ft.×2 ft.

And of the second, she'd had this to say:

> The Girdle—sometimes known as the Cord or the Cingulum—is not merely something to tie around your waist. It is a witch's basic measuring tool. Some witches spin their own material for the Cord, but nowadays most make do with ribbon. Red is the ideal color. After exorcising three 6 ft. 6 in. lengths, the three ends should be tied together and the lengths braided. (For details of ritual, see next chapter.) When the braiding is completed, the three remaining loose ends should be knotted firmly. Other knots should be tied in the Cord as follows: 3 ft. 6 in. from the first knot; then at 4 ft.; 4 ft. 6 in.; 5 ft.; and 5 ft. 6 in. These will be used to measure the radii of the various Magic Circles you will find it necessary to describe.

On the face of it, nothing very hazardous seemed likely to be involved in procuring these articles; but as the time drew near for her to be ticking them off on her list, Alison had begun to realize just how dangerous the task might be.

After all, a table—even a mere two feet by two feet—is still a very large object to transport from one end of the house to the other without being found out.

And as for the Girdle, since ribbon in such quantities was out of the question, considering where she was, only cord would do, or thick string, and—believe it or not—in the whole of that big rambling overfurnished house there wasn't a single ball of string, or even a bunch that was over a couple of feet long.

Alison had searched and searched and had just come to the conclusion that she would have to go around and snip lengths of cord from all the pictures and mirrors and hope that when joined they would produce the necessary nineteen and a half feet, when it came to her just where there might be—would be—almost certainly *was*—a big enough ball of string. It probably wasn't red, of course. That would be too much to hope for, and anyway she'd already had an idea for getting around that problem. But it would be thick enough. She was prepared to stake all three of her Witch Names on that. The only snag was that the place she had in mind was the garden toolshed, and that was where the peril came in.

Ordinarily there would have been nothing to it, but

for a girl still in her dressing gown, able to move about indoors without arousing much comment, but forbidden to go out for another two days or so, the thirty-foot walk (or run, or slink, or crawl) to the shed, along the side of the putting lawn, was like a journey to the farthest reaches of the Amazon.

It had to be thought about.

It was the table problem that Alison tackled first, about two hours after lunch, when the house was at its quietest. In her earlier sorties, she had seen just the thing: one of a stack of card tables in a corner of the basement playroom. She had picked it up and tested it and was glad to find it light enough to carry quite easily, even (she decided) up three flights of stairs. But it was its bulk that looked like making things so difficult. Articles like empty jars or candles or charcoal blocks could be taken up in small batches in the pockets of a dressing gown as easy as anything. Even items as large as the chafing dish could be tucked away under its folds. But a card table—no.

So all that was left to her was to juggle with times and movements and hope for the best, and as she took stock of the situation it began to come out like one of those math problems involving times of trains and speeds of cars; or water pouring into a tub at such and such a rate and leaking away at another. Thus:

Alison McNair desires to transport a table (T) up three flights of stairs (S), including a second-floor landing (L), without anyone knowing

about it. The people she wishes to avoid are her
mother (M), her father (F), her brother (B),
and her sister (J). The time is 3:00 P.M.

Now: (M) is away from the house at the
moment, taking a golf lesson at the club 2
miles away; (F) has been out all day, since
this is Thursday, when he spends the morning
in his New York office; (B) is still in the
house—just like him—on a nice afternoon like
this, too!—writing a letter in the sun lounge
to one of his numerous girl friends; and (J)
was last seen in the bedroom, sitting up in bed
and drawing pictures of her doll.

Put like that, it didn't seem too bad. But the trouble
was that her mother would be due back from three-
fifteen onwards, while her father could come driving up
at any time. If only that stupid Tom hadn't chosen this,
of all afternoons, to catch up with his letter writing!

Alison waited until three-ten, then decided to risk it.
With a bit of luck, Tom would stick at his writing
and never notice a thing, which is more than she could
hope for if her mother was to come back early. . . .

Down in the basement, she hesitated. Now that the
time had come to make the move she wondered if
she'd chosen the best of the tables, after all. She looked
them over again, decided that one with a blue cloth top
looked in better shape, dragged it out of the stack,
changed her mind, and went back to her first choice:
green-topped. This took up no more than an extra three

or four minutes, but it was a delay that almost proved disastrous.

"Hi," said Tom, coming out of the sun lounge and along the corridor at precisely the moment she emerged from the basement. "What have you got there?"

His blue eyes gave the card table a brief glance, but Alison was quick to notice they had a vague, faraway look and that his face was slightly flushed and his fair hair tousled, as if the letter in his hand had caused him no little trouble.

"Just a table," she said, as casually as she could make it sound.

"Oh . . . hmm . . ."

Tom was tapping the envelope on his thumb, still deep in thought. Then he blinked and smiled quickly, as if he'd just noticed again she was there.

"You feeling better now, Sis?"

She winced. If there was one thing she hated about Tom it was his calling her that. Once he used to do it deliberately, knowing it bugged her, but now it was just a habit. Even so, it was something she spat back at him for—as a rule.

Now, however, she just tightened her lips, then forced a smile. This was one time when she wanted him to stay absentminded.

"Oh, fine!" she said. "Much better."

"Hmm . . . great . . ." He flipped the envelope again and frowned. Whatever he'd been writing, she divined (with a certainty that was almost witchlike in itself) that he was feeling guilty about his dealings with girls. "You want me to give you a hand with that, Sis?"

There!

"Thanks all the same," she said, again as casually as she could, "but it's very light."

If he picked it up and moved it somewhere it would be an action, and actions are remembered far more clearly than words. Best to keep it just to words.

"Oh . . . well . . . It's time I was getting this down to the post office. . . . See you, Sis."

Alison sighed deeply as she watched him go. Then, quickly, quietly, not pausing for any rest, she carried off her booty. For all the impression it had made on Tom the encounter might just as well have never taken place. Why (she smiled), it was exactly as if she'd put him into a trance, as if her powers were so great all she had to do was *wish* a spell upon a person!

The thought sustained her all the way to the secret den she had chosen for herself, on a route that took her perilously close to the attic bedroom. Fortunately, Jeannie was still engrossed in her drawing and didn't come out to see what was going on, and the theory didn't have to be put to the test. . . .

By the time Alison had safely stowed the table away with the jars and the knife, the dish, the goblet, and the rest of the day's trophies, it was well after three-fifteen.

Was it too late for the trip to the shed?

Tom was now out of the way, true; and Jeannie was very unlikely to get wind of what was happening so far away from their bedroom and out of the house at that. But now of course the afternoon had entered the danger zone as far as her mother and father were concerned—to say nothing of the additional danger presented by Mr. Crowther, out in the garden.

But then, she told herself, her calculation of three-fifteen as being the earliest possible time for her mother's return had been based on the cold facts of a sixty-minute lesson starting at two o'clock; and now she came to think of it there was about as much likelihood that Emmeline would come flying into the neighborhood on the back of a dragon, or that the McNairs' old cat Norton would return from the dead, as there was that her mother would come home from the golf club without staying for a gossip. As for her father, well—suppose he did drive up while she was out there? He was more like Tom, unsuspecting, especially when his head was filled with business of his own. Him, most definitely, she could handle.

Which left Mr. Crowther, and that decided it for her. Peeping out of her parents' bedroom window, which had venetian blinds and gave an excellent view of the garden with maximum concealment, she saw—and heard —that the gardener was busy beyond the shed and the vegetable patch, mowing the coarser grass all the way down to the woods. Maybe tomorrow he would be working closer to the shed, on a quieter job that would give less evidence of his whereabouts.

So that was that.

It simply *had* to be now.

Alison's dressing gown wasn't exactly the best of camouflages for a foray into the garden. Its basic color was a bright shimmering turquoise, and although a pattern of roses might have been expected to blend well with the rose beds at the side of the small lawn, it would have had to be a more natural one. These roses, emblazoned on Alison back and front, were each about eight inches across: huge gaudy blossoms in neon orange and yellow and an impossible black. Even Jeannie—if she happened to go into the sitting room and glance out of the window—would be sure to spot her.

And as Alison made her crouching, furtive way down beside the roses, it occurred to her that she'd have been better off swapping the dressing gown for her old green raincoat. But by then she was three quarters of the way to the shed, and she decided she might just as well press on. To return now would be like exposing herself to the maximum danger almost twice the necessary amount of time—for it was only out here that she was in danger of being spotted. In the shed—

Here she cut short that train of thought and concentrated only on what she actually *was* doing. This was because she had reached the door of the shed itself. Only action counted now.

So, quickly, firmly, she turned the handle, pushed, and went into the dusty pine-scented shade. It was crammed with tools and pots and boxes and sacks, but in an orderly way—much more orderly than the kitchen. Along one side ran a long bench and on the other there were wooden racks. Down at the far end of the narrow corridor between the racks and the bench was another door, slightly ajar, leading into another storeroom of some kind. It looked quite pitch black in there, judging from the crack at the edge, but anyway it didn't matter. What Alison had come for lay *there*, just inside the main entrance, at eye level: a ball of thick white hairy garden string as big as a pumpkin, with a cluster of reserves behind it.

"Bless you, Mr. Grouch—I mean Crowther—for being such an orderly man."

So saying, Alison took the leading ball from the shelf, tucked it into the top of her dressing gown, wriggled sharply and laughed as it gave her neck a scratchy tickle, and drew one of the reserve balls from the back.

The thought of Mr. Crowther made her turn her head to the door and listen. She smiled and sighed with relief and satisfaction. The mower was still buzzing away out there, its rhythms good and steady and regular.

She began to look around her more calmly. Several times that day she had noticed articles which, though not down on her list, looked as if they might come in handy during the witching nights ahead. Now that she was there—in a treasure house second only to the kitchen complex—maybe she'd see something that—

Her heart gave a thump.

Of course!

Oh, but this was too much!

Dare she?

She had caught sight of a broom—a beautiful, raggedy, bristly broom, a genuine, old-fashioned, authentic, regular Witch's Broom—leaning in a far corner, by the second door.

She approached it slowly. She fingered it gingerly, as if expecting it to take off at a touch, out through the door and over the startled Crowther, with her still clinging to it.

Its handle was not very long, no more than three feet or so. It was formed from a dull soft wood, grimy, much used. The surface was irregular but nowhere sharp or splintery. When she picked it up, it seemed to press itself comfortably, snugly, into her palms, so that for a second or two she thought it really might be impossible ever to put it down again. Its bristles sang scratchily like an old record as she gave it a gentle swing (and how willingly it responded in its swing!) across the boards of the floor. Much sweat had gone into the pores of the wood of that handle to soften it and make it as supple as this, she thought—and for a moment she was struck with the notion of another kind of magic, a magic belonging to Crowther himself and other workmen like him, and she thought of the expression "green fingers"— and then it passed, this notion of an ordinary, everyday, unspectacular kind of magic, and she was back with her own.

Should she or should she not take the broom back with her?

Mr. Crowther would be sure to miss it.

But what better trophy could there be, what better reward for her boldness, what better boldness-bonus than this?

What would Ariadne M. have done?

Alison closed her eyes, hoping to hear some murmur of

Yes or No from the shade of her predecessor. But all was silent, all was—

Silent?

Again she felt her heart lurch.

And yes—the motor outside had stopped.

Did that mean she was in danger of being discovered? She put down the broom and began to tiptoe to the door. She had gone only halfway when a shadow crossed a dull-glassed window behind the racks, and she heard the clump of feet.

Hugging the ball of string, she turned and scampered back to the end of the shed, pulling open the second door and stumbling into the dark recess beyond it. Then she crouched there, pulling the door to and breathing as softly as she could, through her mouth, listening.

Mr. Crowther was obviously an inveterate talker-to-himself, and he was already in the middle of a long conversation when he entered the shed.

"And whatsa use of having a game warden then, tell me *that?*" he was saying. "Huh? How 'bout that, huh? Eh? Whyn't you answer me that, if you can, huh?"

Alison shut her eyes as the footsteps clumped nearer and nearer along the boards.

"You just take your time about it, there's no hurry, but you just tell me whatsa use of having a game warden if that's his attitude. You just be thinking around *that*, while I—"

Here came a grunting and scraping sound.

"—take this here can of gasoline and fill old Graywings up."

Alison blinked. Could he really mean the mower? *Graywings?* She was beginning to wonder just who *was* the witch around here.

Then she listened hard again as the footsteps retreated and the muttering was resumed.

"Tell you one thing. They won't get *me* goin' to no meeting. . . ."

The outer door closed and the muttering and the footsteps were muffled.

"Give him two minutes, just in case he changes his mind and comes back for something," Alison whispered to herself, aloud, sufficiently impressed by the man's habit to try it out on herself. "If he doesn't return by then you'll know he's busy filling—er—Graywings, and that'll be the safest time."

So she waited, and as she did so, she found her eyes had become accustomed to the darkness of her hiding place. It was—she felt around—some kind of special storeroom with racks of shallow trays lining the wall behind her. Nuts and bolts, were they—as in similar trays in Daddy's workroom back home? Spare parts for the mower, for Grayw—

She had been fumbling gently as she wondered, and what had caused her to break off this time was the recognition that had gone tingling up from the tips of her fingers.

Bulbs!

This was where Mr. Crowther stored them.

Rapidly now, her fingers flitted from tray to tray, touching the cool, hard, smooth flower bulbs, feeling their irregularities, testing for size.

Then:

"Great!" she said, softly but explosively. "These will be *perfect!*"

As she filled her pockets with the bulbs, she made up her mind about the broomstick. Regretfully, no. It really would be too quickly missed. And Mr. Crowther would be sure to feel bad about the disappearance of something as useful to him as that. Why, he probably had a name for it too. *Bristles* or something. Or *Browntail.* But Bristles or Browntail had served its magical purpose anyway, so she didn't feel so bad about relinquishing the broomstick. It had done its work by leading her to the bulbs like this. For now she had the makings of that most important item of all: her Witch's Necklace.

Even as she let the bulbs run through her fingers in the darkness of her pockets, she knew exactly what she would do. She would coat them with nail varnish before threading them. That would preserve them beautifully, containing under a thin crust all the color and bursting irresistible power of springtime, holding it for her personal use in the black midnights ahead.

She felt elated, so confident in the power of the bulbs—unvarnished and unthreaded though they were as yet—that she didn't even bother to stoop or run as she returned to the house up the side of the rose beds. Nobody would see her, she told herself—no matter who looked out of a window or came scrunching up the driveway. The power of the bulbs would take care of that!

Well, be that as it may, it has to be recorded that nobody *did* see her, and she slipped indoors unchallenged, a considerable number of steps farther along the path to witchhood.

CHAPTER 7

Secrets

"And so she now had all the main things—the most important main things anyway—and she was all set."

In the darkness, against a background chorus of crickets again, Alison was continuing her series of bedtime stories about Ariadne, the Beginner Witch.

"All—all set?"

Jeannie sounded as if she was trying to sound not as puzzled as she really sounded.

Alison smiled happily. It was good to have a sister as dumb as Jeannie. Someone to whom you could tell so much and thereby relieve the pressure of a whole day's gathering of juicy secrets, without being in danger of actually giving them away.

"Yes," she said, not bothering to hide her glee at the prospect ahead of her, "all set to cast spells, and gaze into the future, and make magical happenings, and raise the dead, and—"

"Raise the *dead?*"

"Oh, yes! We witches—all good witches can do that, you know."

"Ugh! It sounds—"

"And change the weather—did you know witches can do *that?* Raise mighty storms, make it rain, make it calm, make it snow. . . . And they can punish their enemies without even going near them, and—and they can make people like them without having to go to all the bother of being nice to them."

"Boys?"

"Yes, boys as well, of course, anybody, male or female, old or young . . . Say, what *is* all this with you and boys? You're too young always to be thinking about boys."

"Well, so are you and Emmeline then!"

"Oh, well, if you're going to start *that* again—"

"No! Sorry. Go on about the witch-girl, Alison, please. What did Harry Adny do next?"

"There you go again! Boys on the brain! It *isn't* Harry anything. How many more times? It's Ariadne. Got it? Ari—A, R, I—adne—A, D, N, E."

"Sorry . . . It's such a stupid name, it—"

"Have a care!"

"Eh?"

Jeannie sounded uneasy, and no wonder. Alison's voice had seemed to come from the grave itself. It continued that way, too:

"I said have ye a care, lest the spirit that lurks in every Witch Name should be offended!"

"Oh, no, Alison! Please! Please don't talk in that voice, not in the dark. You know I—"

"Well, just watch it then. O.K.?"

"Yes. O.K., Alison. Sorry."

Alison smiled severely and said:

"I should think so, too. I mean, you don't think I *like* having my voice taken over by a witch's spirit, do you? I mean, if you go and insult it, it gets back at the insulter through the one who's telling the story about it. And that's me."

"Oh!"

"Yes, 'Oh!' . . . Anyway, about Ariadne and all the things she collected that day. Well. There were more."

"More things? But you said she'd got all the main things."

"So I did. But there were extras. You know what Daddy's always saying. To be really good at your job, to be top, the boss, the superstar, it's the extras you put into it. And I—I mean Ariadne—she certainly had an eye open for the extras. She was very bright, you know, as well as being very—oh, *ravishingly*—beautiful."

"What sort of extras?"

"Well, there was the knife rack. . . ."

"Knife rack?"

"Yes. One of those magnetic ones, like a thin strip of wood you screw onto walls and the knives just stick to it. The black-handled knife she found in the muddly old kitchen was on one of them."

"But what use could that be to a witch?"

"Heh! heh! You'd be very surprised, deary, to know just what *would* be of use to a witch."

"Alison, *please!* Don't talk in that scratchy voice, please. I didn't insult whatsername that time, did I?"

"No. I'm sorry. Anyway—"

"It makes me go all shivery. And when you call me 'deary' with it, it's even worse."

"Anyway," continued Alison, softly now, and dreamily, "this knife rack. It wasn't a very big one. And it was all lopsided, with only one screw holding it to the wall at one end and the other one missing. It was as easy as anything to get it off the wall. She used the tip of the knife. The screw that was in wasn't very tight, you see."

"But what use would the knife rack *be?*"

"I've told you. You'd be surprised what use a good witch can put a thing to."

"Well, what use did she *think* it would be? She must have thought *something*, to make her take it like that."

"Witches don't need to think. Sometimes they just feel. Ariadne just *felt* it would be useful and then—*shazzam!*—even while she was unscrewing it, she *knew.*"

"What? Knew what?"

"You'll have to wait for another night to hear about that."

"But I want to know—"

"And then there was the black paint and the glass plate. Actually, she saw the glass plate first, one of those thick glass dinner plates you can put in the stove, and she felt that it might be useful, but not very strongly did she feel it, so she left it. And then later she saw the black paint, a small can, and she felt *that* might be useful also, but again she didn't feel very strongly. And she was going to leave that too, and then she remembered not feeling very strongly about the glass plate, so she thought about them both together, black paint and glass plate, and then she *did* feel very strongly, and she knew exactly what to do with them, and—"

"What? What did she know to do with them?"

"And so she took them," continued Alison, almost hypnotized by her own story and its ebbing and flowing in the darkness, on a sea of chanting crickets. "And then she saw the wine, a dirty old bottle, all dusty, standing on the floor in a dark corner of one of the pantry closets, nearly full of red port wine and she took that, because she had a feeling about that also."

"Did she drink it?"

"No! Stupid! It wasn't for drinking she felt she had a use for it."

"What then? And I'm *not* stupid! How do I know what some stupid w—"

"Ah-ah! She'll hear you!"

"Well . . . I'm sorry. . . . But what *did* she want the wine for, Alison?"

"For that, you'll have to wait for another night's story. It's late. Go to sleep. Goodnight."

There was no answer.

Alison heard Jeannie breathing hard, almost grunting —the way she always sounded when she was grappling with a weighty problem. Weighty for *her*, of course . . .

Then:

"Alison?"

"Yes?"

"Where did she hide it all? Where did she have her den? I mean all these things—the table, the jars, charcoal, salt. . . . I mean there was such a *lot* of stuff for her to hide, wasn't there?"

Alison's lips tightened in the darkness. Somehow she was not quite sure she liked the sound of that question.

She pretended to yawn.

"Oh well, that's another story. But she'd gotten herself a den all right."

"Yes, but *where?*"

"That's another story. . . . Goodnight, Jeannie."

"Was it—?"

"Goodnight, Jeannie."

"No, but—"

"Pry not too closely," intoned Alison, in her voice-from-the-grave, "before a secret be ready to be revealed to thee."

"You said you wouldn't talk like that again! You *said!*"

"And you said you'd be careful not to insult or—er—or annoy the spirit of Ariadne. O.K.?"

"I'm sorry. I only—"

"Goodnight, Jeannie."

"Oh, goodnight then!"

Alison smiled in the darkness. She smiled the "enigmatic secret smile" that she'd been practicing ever since she'd read in the book that this was a *sure sign of confident Witchhood.* Trouble was, there was still something she wasn't quite happy about in her sister's tone. Something new. Something that told her she'd perhaps better be a little more careful than usual during the next few crucial days.

CHAPTER 8

Incantation in a High Tower

"Dipped and soaked,
On strong wine fed,
O cord of power,
Come thou out red!"

Alison was very proud of her incantation. It was the first she had made up for herself, and it was the first to be put to practical use. No wonder her voice trembled a little as—naked except for her black poncho with the deep blue stars, a somewhat sticky homemade necklace of thirteen nail-varnished hyacinth bulbs, and her red rubber garter with its brass bell attachment—she began prancing around her worktable in the den she had refused to describe to Jeannie the night before.

It was very small and bare and grimy, this place, but otherwise ideal. For one thing, it was six-sided, perfectly hexagonal in shape, and this seemed to Alison to be very propitiously witchlike indeed. What was more, it was actually a tower, which in her view put it right at the top of the magical habitations class. Admittedly it wasn't made of glass or crystal—being simply a brick and timber extension to the rest of the house, placed at a corner of the roof for largely decorative purposes. But it did have a satisfactorily conical roof and, with its three dirt-caked slit windows, a satisfactorily sinister look, especially when seen from the outside.

"What hideous monstrosities!" Mrs. McNair had said, months ago, when the family had come to look over the house on a particularly dull Sunday.

And even Alison had had to agree, as she gazed up at the twin gray-green peaks, like horns, one at either side of the front of the house, with ragged black clouds streaming behind them.

"I mean, what *use* are they? What rooms can be as small as *that?*" Mrs. McNair had gone on to ask.

And:

"None at all, ma'am," had replied Mrs. Crowther, who'd been showing them around and looking as grouchy as her husband. "They was just put there to look pretty. I kind of like them myself."

Nobody had bothered to ask how you got into them. Mr. and Mrs. McNair just hadn't been interested enough, and Alison had taken it for granted that they would come across the entrances when they were looking around inside. And then, when the time had come for that, there'd been so many real rooms to wander in and out of and criticize or praise that even she had quite forgotten about the towers.

When she had decided to become a witch, however, her interest had suddenly revived, with a crackle and tingle that were almost electric.

"Of course!" she had gasped, after combing her

brains for a good location for a den, and getting no
farther than a corner of the basement. "Of course!"
she had repeated, in her imagination soaring so high, so
fast, from cellar to rooftop, that for an instant she felt
quite giddy. "The towers! I'll use one for spells and one
for curses!"

But when she'd come to track down their entrances
she'd had to modify those plans, for to find the way into
just one of them was baffling enough, while the other
had either been bricked and plastered up long since or
had never been anything more than a solid dummy
right from the building of the house.

Still, one would be sufficient after all. Especially one
as convenient and—and *witchy*—as this, she decided
when, with a tingling again, she had pushed open the
creaking door and looked into its dimness for the very
first time: at the six walls, with the slit windows high
in the three that faced the door, and the narrow shelf,
really a ledge, that ran around the room at shoulder
height on five of the sides.

The room had been bare but thick with dust and
veiled with cobwebs. Apart from clearing the shelf of
its coating—by scraping if off with a handkerchief—
she let the place remain in this condition. Then, item
by item, she had brought in the implements and jewels
of her new career—furtively, silently, feeling pretty sure
that once she'd conveyed them within those six walls her
secret would be safe forever.

Because that was the best of all about her tower den:
its splendid concealment from prying eyes or blundering
feet inside the house. Who—she asked herself—would

bother to look beyond the opening of the closet, small, square, dark, on the landing outside the sitting room and the bedroom in the attic? After all, not many people, unless they were specially looking, would even notice the door, which had been covered with a rose-patterned paper, now faded, like the rest of the wall, and was given away only by the faint cracks around its sides and along its top and by one small black knob.

Why, Alison herself, on her first morning in the house, had done no more than glance in the closet and note the old trunk and suitcase that had been left, and shrug, and close the door. True, she'd just been sickening with the measles then, feeling drowsy and dull and wondering what was wrong with her and certainly in no mood for exploring. Yet even so, she firmly believed that a sick Alison was equal to at least three healthy alert ordinaries —and this gave her a great glow of security when she did get around to investigating further and found that the closet extended in an L-shape beyond the dark left-hand corner, into a place of strange gurglings and hiss-ings, where the huge water tank was kept.

Who but she would ever get this far, unless it was a plumber come to fix some defect? Her mother? With all that dust and grime? Ridiculous! Her father or Tom? No chance. The menfolk of that family weren't in the least interested in exploring old houses just for kicks. Jeannie, then? (And this was the real test, *theoretically* the biggest danger.) Laughable!

Jeannie, with her fear of any strange room or closet and her dread of dark corners would never even make it into the first chamber, let alone the water tank

part. Why, if Alison had *wanted* her to go that far,
and had promised to come with her and hold her hand
and go first, Jeannie would still have required a whole
morning's heavy persuading, with half a dozen tiptoe
trials. So how could there ever be a risk of her going
even farther, squeezing past the tank to the dark wall
beyond, with its darker door—the entrance to the tower?

Ariadne Atropos Arachne felt so sure of these things
that her step became livelier and her chanting a little
louder as she pranced around the table that morning.

> "Dipped and soaked,
> On strong wine fed,
> O cord of power,
> Come thou out red!"

The floor around the table had been cleared of everything save the dust, which she now began to raise in
small puffs, as around and around she danced, the brass
bell above her left knee faintly jingling, and the necklace
bulbs swaying and clumping against her bare chest
under the poncho. On the shelf along one wall the row
of jars and bottles winked at her as she whirled past
them. On the next section the unlit candles lay in
another businesslike row, the wax softly gleaming and
the end ones reflected in the silvery sheen of the chafing
dish at the end of the next section. Beside the chafing
dish, the charcoal blocks stirred occasionally as a corner
of the poncho flicked their bulging paper sack; while
on the next section the jar of salt gleamed brighter
than bottles or dish, and harsher than the candles.

Strangest brightness of all, however, was that at the back
of the glass plate, coated with glossy black paint from
the can beside it, and propped to dry on the shelf next
to the door.

But these were objects and reflections seen from the
eye corners only, as Alison whirled and pranced and
chanted: a circular background of sheens and glitters,
glimmers and glows, shimmerings and twinklings. Her
conscious attention was focused increasingly on the table,
in the center of which was the large glass goblet, filled
with port wine and a length of the purloined garden
string which lay coiled in its bottom.

"Dipped and soaked!" sang Alison, prodding the string
lightly with the tip of the black-handled knife, which was
acting as a kind of pivot.

"Soaked and dipped!" she sang, trying to lift the string
a little, as if it were spaghetti on the end of a fork.

"On strong wine fed, fed on strong wine!"

True to form, she was growing tired of repeating herself, was warming to her subject, was getting carried
away.

"O cord of power, turn red, turn red!"

Then she remembered herself and lowered her voice
and prodded the lurching goblet less dangerously and
resumed the original chant.

> "Dipped and soaked,
> On strong wine fed,
> O cord of power,
> Come thou out red!"

And she was just wondering—wandering a little in her mind, against all the rules laid down by the author of *The Secret Arts of Witchcraft*—whether Ariadne M. had ever used this wonderful tower-den herself, when, through the chanting, the jingling, and the clumping and from the dark gap in the outer circle of gleams, glisterings, shinings, and sheens, there came a peculiar squeak and a gasp, and the weird unearthly croak of her name:

"Alison!"

CHAPTER 9

The Beginning of a Coven?

Such an interruption, in such a voice, at such a critical moment, in such a supposedly remote and secret place, was bad enough. If Ariadne herself had appeared, flanked by such awful Dark Powers as Hecate and the Lord Vassago—horned, fanged, taloned, and out for blood—Alison couldn't have been more deeply shocked and chilled.

But when she wheeled around, dropping the knife with a thud on the table, and saw the face that was staring at her, pale as the candles, eyes wide and staring, and recognized it, she nearly fainted.

"Jeannie!" she gasped. "How—? What—? Jeannie! *You!*"

If anything, Jeannie's face was registering greater shock than her own. But Jeannie's shock was obviously not so much at finding Alison there as at finding her so strangely dressed and in such weird surroundings.

"What—what are you doing, Alison?" she whispered, still clinging to the handle of the door, cobwebs in her hair and all over the shoulders and sleeves of her yellow pajamas.

Alison gulped back exactly the same question. What in the world, she was wondering, was Jeannie doing there, against all her calculations? How had she ever found the courage to get beyond the first closet, past the trunk and the suitcase, around the corner, and through the webs and shadows of the cistern chamber to the door of the tower? Alison decided there and then that it must have been something to do with the measles. Maybe a gland had been damaged, destroying Jeannie's usually high-powered sense of caution.

She began to look at the younger girl with fresh interest, even as her annoyance began to well up.

"How did you know where to find me?" she asked.

"I—I watched. . . . I saw you take your poncho out of the drawer, and I wondered what you wanted it for and—and I watched through the keyhole into the sitting room and I saw you take your dressing gown off and then your nightdress and hide them behind the bookcase, and then put the poncho on. And—I just wondered. . . ."

"Why, you—you disgusting little spy!"

Jeannie screamed sharply, for Alison had stamped and in so doing had rung the bell on her garter.

This made Alison feel better.

"So then I suppose you watched from the *sitting-room* keyhole?"

"Oh, no—no, honestly, Alison!"

Jeannie was staring at the corner of the poncho from which the electrifying ringing had come.

Alison stamped again and rejoiced to see her sister flinch once more at the trill of the bell.

"Then how did you get to know where I'd gone?"

"I—I saw you through the crack in the door. It was partly open."

"Keyhole, crack—what does it matter? You were spying, you—you loathsome little creep!"

"Well, you shouldn't sneak about like that! You're the creepy one!"

The brown eyes caught sight of the knife on the table. A spot of wine glistened near the point. The eyes widened, then wavered.

"What's that for? Is that—that isn't—it isn't *blood* in that glass, is it?"

"Mind your own business."

"It isn't though, is it?"

Jeannie looked ready to run, screaming the house down. Regretfully, Alison decided it would be more prudent to allay her fears.

"No, of course not."

"What is it? Is it wine?"

"Yes. Now—"

"Port wine? The wine you were telling me about last night?"

Jeannie's eyes had been ranging around the shelves. She looked more sure of herself now. The color was coming back to her cheeks. She turned to Alison and smiled faintly.

"*You're* Ariadne, aren't you?"

All right, buster! thought Ariadne Atropos Arachne. *You've asked for this!*

"Yes," she said, in her crackiest, croakiest witch voice. "She I be!" And she stamped thrice, making the bell ring as she uttered each word. "And thou I shalt put a curse upon for defiling this mine most secret tower!"

Jeannie screamed and spun around.

"Oh, come back, come back!" said Alison quickly, in her normal voice. "I didn't mean it. Besides," she added, noticing how Jeannie had stopped in her tracks and turned again and was glancing over her shoulder into the cistern chamber, "you might take the wrong turning through there and end up with the bats in the rafters."

"Bu-bats?"

"Yes. Bats. Not *quite* as bad as vampires, but—"

"Oh, Alison, please come with me!"

"You were bold enough to come after me alone."

"Yes, but—but I didn't know how spooky it was till I was there, here, at the door."

"You should have thought of that before."

Jeannie's eyes were roving again, her fear subsiding under a fresh wave of curiosity.

"Are those the bulbs? Around your neck? The ones you said she took from the garden shed?"

"What do they look like?" said Alison, playing for time, thinking fast. "Baseballs?"

"You *are* Ariadne, aren't you though? The girl in the Beginner Witch stories?"

Alison had made up her mind. It cost her a lot to do it, but she just had to play the whole thing down if she didn't want Jeannie to go blabbering hysterically to their mother.

"It—it's just a game," she said.

Jeannie sighed. It was a huge sigh, seeming to well up from her toes, lifting her shoulders.

"A witch game?"

"A witch game."

Alison waited, watching with concealed dismay the confidence go surging through her sister's frame. She had a good idea what would be coming next.

And it did.

"Can *I* play, Alison?"

Alison tried out a faint hope.

"You should be in bed still."

"I shouldn't, I shouldn't! Momma said I could get up and move around more today if I kept improving."

"You look very pale."

"I always do. It's my hair. *You* do. . . . Please, Alison, let me play at witches with you."

Alison groaned softly and shook her leg, sounding a faint knell for the death of her weakling hope.

"And can I see how you make that ringing?" added Jeannie eagerly, stooping, not in the least scared of it now.

"Later," said Alison. "Just stay quite still and be quiet while I think about it."

Dutifully, Jeannie did as she was told, straightening up and even putting her arms behind her back and her chest out, as if trying to impress a teacher.

And so, in the hexagonal tower, her violated lair, her discovered den, Alison considered the situation.

What, she asked herself, would happen if she refused Jeannie's application, as she would dearly—oh, so very dearly!—have loved to do?

A row, of course. A blabbering to their mother, almost certainly. A constant harassment, perpetual spying, end-less interruptions—these went without saying. And an-other den would have to be found, that was for sure.

That side of the question looked black, black as the back of that glass plate, which she'd so been looking forward to seeing the future in. . . .

She sighed, then frowned at Jeannie as her sister's mouth began to open. The mouth closed obediently.

Well, that was one thing about the kid. She knew when it paid her to do as she was told, to keep her mouth shut, to be content with holding onto the tag ends of her older sister's flying imagination. . . .

I mean—Alison told herself—it's not as though she'll have an important part to play.

Yet even so, she could be very useful.

And after all, it was more fun, having someone on hand to admire you and the brilliant successes you were bound to have.

Besides—witches did work together. This could even be the beginning of a coven! Why, she needn't wait now for that, as she'd intended—holding it off until they returned to New York and she could swear Emmeline in.

And, to crown all, didn't Jeannie also have red hair, even if it wasn't the same rich resonant shade as her own? I mean—she thought—*two* red-haired witches would mean almost double the power.

Jeannie, watching her face, was smiling faintly again.

So long as she did exactly as she was told, Alison added mentally.

Jeannie's smile faded.

Which she *would*, of course, decided Alison, confident in the skill of her sistercraft, which had been tested far longer than her witchcraft, and had come through with flying colors so very many times. . . .

"All right," she said crisply. "You're in."

"Oh, great!" cried Jeannie. "Can *I* have a—"

"So long as you remember this: that it isn't all *that* much of a game."

"Excuse me?"

"I mean, it's a very *serious* game. O.K.?"

"Yes, sure. Can—?"

"And you have to do exactly what I tell you and remember at all times you're just a student witch, under me."

"Why can't I be a proper witch, a—a *graduate* witch?"

"You want to cut your arm and write out a full witch's oath in your own blood?" asked Alison mildly, reaching for the knife.

"Oh—I—do you have to do that?"

"That's the only *short* way," said Alison, with such glibness that she was almost convincing herself she'd read it in the book. "Otherwise it's a steady six months' apprenticeship. Being an apprentice witch. Get it? A Deputy Witch. *My* Deputy."

"Oh, well—all right—sure . . ."

Alison put the knife back on the table, and Jeannie's face cleared.

"Good," said Alison. "So that's settled."

She pulled an end of the string from the wine and frowned. It was terribly pale compared to the color of the wine which was so rich and strong-looking. But it was better than if it had remained white. And maybe if they *both* chanted the incantation the dye would take quicker.

"Jeannie," she said, "don't thee mind now about my witchy voice. Just try to make thine sound the same."

"I—you mean—?" Slowly, a delighted grin spread over Jeannie's face. "Like thee thisee?"

Alison groaned.

"Not so much of the ee's and a lot scratchier."

"I—I do not think—oh, *that* was better, though, was it not, thinks thee?"

"Terrific, sister!" cackled Alison, patting Jeannie on the shoulder and shaking a veritable peal of joy from her left leg. "Now say thou this after me. . . ."

Thus, slowly at first, then with more confidence, and finally with gleeful abandon, the Deputy Witch joined her sister in the prancing chant around the table.

> "Dipped and soaked,
> On strong wine fed,
> O cord of power,
> Come thou out red!"

CHAPTER 10

Mirror, Mirror . . .

Over the next two weeks or so the progress in witch-craft of Ariadne Atropos Arachne and her Deputy (who'd been granted the single, *provisional* Witch Name of her choice: *Jezebel,* of all things) went side by side with the progress of their recovery. True enough, Mrs. McNair had certain doubts on this second score, making from time to time such comments as:

"Your eyes seem to have survived all right, but what on earth has the measles done to your voices, all this croaki-ness you both keep breaking into?"

And later:

"I can't understand you guys, really I can't. Now that the doctor says you *can* go outdoors, you seem to spend half your time up in the attic!"

But Mrs. McNair wasn't the superfussy type, and so long as the girls ate their meals and *looked* more like their normal healthy selves, she didn't go clucking around them, checking on everything they did. After all, they were on vacation, herself included, and now that they were medically well out of any danger she took the opportunity of stepping up her golf lessons and spending more time visiting around.

This suited the witches fine, for there was much to be done at that stage. There was, for instance, the Consecration of the Tools—the equipment already garnered by Alison. And there was the assembly of a basic kit for Jeannie—not as full as Alison's, nor anything near as elaborate, but, as the older girl promised: "A good basic starter kit, to be going on with, until you're ready to graduate."

Oddly enough, and to Alison's great relief, Jeannie didn't seem to mind this much, accepting a garterless, workbookless, girdleless, knifeless beginning without a murmur, and being quite content with a necklace of a mere five varnished bulbs, the remainder of Alison's original stock. Then again, maybe it wasn't all that odd, Alison reflected after a while, noting her sister's impatience to be getting on with the consecrating procedures.

For this was a beautifully messy, truly witchy activity even when they didn't go exactly by the book—which was often—which was in fact *very* often—which was, to tell the truth, nearly always. It meant spending hours up in the tower, sometimes after dark. It meant—with the consecrating of the goblet, for instance—mixing salt and water and whispering magical incantations while adding pinches of sage and mint. The book had asked that about a dozen other herbs and spices be included, most of which the girls had never heard of and at least two of which had names they couldn't pronounce.

But Alison had gotten around this in her usual way,

by improvising. Thus she used spoonfuls of detergent
(borrowing some of the words printed on the packet
to form a brand-new incantation, incorporating such
phrases as "active-enzyme" and "lemon-freshened").
Pinches of bath salts she used, too, with additional dashes
of talcum powder—which last she also used as incense,
sprinkling it over the charcoal blocks she heated on a
bed of sand in the chafing dish.

"Blessed be . . . blessed be . . ."

These were the words most often murmured in the
secret chamber beyond the water tank, during those
sessions.

"Blessed be thou, cup of magical waters. . . ."

Or:

"Blessed be thou, bowl of fire. . . ."

Or:

"Blessed be thou, knife of steel. . . ."

Or:

"Let *me* blessed-be something, please, Alison!"

Or:

"I was just going to, only you've spoiled it for
tonight by not calling me my Witch Name!"

So incantations were murmured (or, as Ariadne Atropos Arachne preferred it, incantations were *breathed*);
and objects sprinkled with salty scummy water and passed
through sometimes barely visible, sometimes thick and
choking, fumes of "incense." So, on completion of
such preliminaries, objects were marked with the magic
letters

чуч

which, according to the book, were the initials AAA in
the runic alphabet, the witch's own.

"But it says you've to write other things in that
squiggly code also," Jeannie had protested once, at the
beginning. "Something special for each of the things."

"Unnecessary," said Alison to that. She remembered
an exasperating few minutes she'd spent trying to scratch
the appropriate inscription on the glass goblet, before
settling for a felt-penned triple-A. "The witch who wrote
the book was also a teacher," she explained, recalling
her thoughts on that very first afternoon, about the doubtful necessity for a small engraving knife, and finding these
thoughts to have hardened into facts in the meantime.
"She couldn't *help* fussing, I suppose. But we don't
have to go along with it so long as our feelings are
strong enough and vivid enough. . . . Pass me that
packet of sage and let's get on with the consecrating."

And then, with everything duly (more or less) con-
secrated and the witches all tooled-up for action, there
came the glorious period of the Pendulum and the
Magic Mirror.

These were the fun things. They were not as complicated as spells and—as the girls were soon to find
out—they were infinitely more satisfying to operate. This
was because, being mainly concerned with such open-
ended mysteries as character reading and fortune-telling,
any failure was never immediately apparent and one-
hundred-percent successes could be claimed time after
time. Granted, there *would* come a day when the reading
or prediction *might* be proved wrong, but as Ariadne
Atropos Arachne pointed out to Jezebel more than once:

"What kind of a witch are you, if you don't *know* you're right, right at the start, without waiting for proof? Of *course* it'll come true!"

The Pendulum was one of Alison's major triumphs. To form the weight, the book had called for a lodestone, and even when she remembered that all this really meant was a magnet, Alison had been baffled for a time.

"Where can I get a magnet from, stuck here, in this place?" she had muttered, frowning at the yellow-edged page. "Now, if we were back home . . ."

But not being back home, and being nothing if not practical, Alison had dismissed the Pendulum from her mind until, during her early foray in the kitchen, she had discovered the magnetic knife rack.

"Of course!" she had murmured then, turning away at its remaining screw with the point of the knife. "It's even got a hole all ready-made to put the string through."

There again—in the matter of material to suspend the magnet by—she had triumphed. This time it was not so much a question of triumph over adversity, either, because there was no shortage of string after her visit to the garden shed, of course. No; this time it was a direct triumph over the author of the book.

"*Hold out your Pendulum over a piece of paper on which you have inscribed your question,*" the instructions read. "*If the answer be Yea, the Pendulum will swing to and fro. But if the answer be Nay, from side to side will the Pendulum swing.*"

Yet using string, the main reaction had been neither side to side nor to and fro, but an infuriating spinning, generally counterclockwise.

"Why don't we say that when it spins that way the answer is Yes?" Jeannie had asked, noting her sister's frown.

"Because it looks as if it'll nearly always spin that way, and we want a fifty-fifty chance of Yes or No. I mean, we might want to ask it if Mom's really going to make us take piano lessons this fall, the way she's been threatening to."

Then inspiration had come, and Alison had gone down into the kitchen and had returned ten minutes later with a card of bright shiny fuse wire.

"*That* won't twizzle around," she had said.

And she'd been right.

Whether the motions of the knife rack at the end of the wire turned out to be exactly fifty Yeses to fifty Noes per hundred, it would be unscientific to say, since nobody kept count. But it did seem to work out roughly like that, after an initial doubtful patch in which Yeses predominated. This early bias was probably because the questions during that first period were laid face up, with the questioner doing her own divining.

Thus it was Yes to Alison's *Shall I soon be able to turn iron into gold?*—and Yes again to *Will they let us have another cat to replace Norton?*—and a positively vigorously swinging Yes to *Will I marry a terrifically handsome man, just like Ben Murphy, who won't mind my continuing to be a witch?*

Similarly, there had been a whole series of Yeses to Jeannie's questions, concerning such topics as would Sylvie ever be able to walk again, and would there be chocolate chip ice cream again for lunch, and would

she get married very young, and would it (here the
Pendulum bucked and kicked its assent) be to a young
man just like that boy in the Carpenters. . . .

"I think," said Alison thoughtfully at this point, "we
might be giving it a bit of help without really knowing
it."

"Oh, no!" said Jeannie. "I'm sure it's just telling us
the way things will be, truthfully."

"Well, let's try it another way then. Why don't we
try not letting each other know what's on the paper,
turning it upside down, and letting the other one do
the holding?"

This method very quickly restored the balance, with
many more Noes beginning to crop up. And while
Jeannie suffered a number of shocks and disappoint-
ments, as a result of continuing to ask questions to which
she desired Yes answers (that way she lost her early
marriage at the second time of asking), Alison's deep
mind quickly adjusted. She too had an occasional shock
(like Yes, she would soon be in a situation of the very
greatest danger—and Yes, she would be lucky to escape
with her life)—but these were pleasant shocks mainly,
and they were most happily balanced by a series of juicy
Noes, such as the one about the piano lessons, and
another that reassured her there would be no treatment
required on her next visit to the dentist.

"Alison," said Jeannie, after a particularly disappoint-
ing reply to a question about the likelihood of her getting
for Christmas a twenty-room, all-electric, sliding-roofed,
fully-furnished doll's house she'd seen in a New York
store and had been dearly coveting for months, "why

is it that this way it's nearly always good answers for you and bad answers for me?"

Alison shrugged.

"Fate, I suppose."

"What d'you mean?"

"Don't worry, honey. It means you're like one of those beautiful characters in books and movies that everything goes wrong with and we feel so sorry for we could cry."

"I—I don't *wanna* be one of them! I—I think you're cheating."

"Now how can I—when you're the one who holds the Pendulum for my questions? I mean, it's not as if I stand anywhere near you. I mean, how can I nudge you or anything and cause a tilt the way you can cheat a pinball machine. I mean, come *on*, Jezebel!"

But the time had arrived to give her Deputy's spirits a boost, Alison could see that, and so she quickly turned their attention to the Magic Mirror.

This was much less liable to "tilting"—conscious or otherwise. And indeed it did give Jeannie's spirits a lift, even though Alison hadn't anticipated just how great it would be—how high it would send Jeannie's confidence soaring, to say nothing of her own respect for her kid sister's potential as a witch. . . .

The Magic Mirror was made from the glass plate, which Alison had painted black on its underside, and an old wooden salad bowl. According to the book, the plate should have been a clock glass and the salad bowl a specially made slab of wood, hollowed out in the middle. But Alison had neither the tools nor the patience to produce the pedestal in the prescribed way, and was completely baffled as to where she could get hold of a clock glass without doing serious damage to the household's timepieces. So she settled instead for the plate and the salad bowl (also found in the kitchen) and made up for her lack of patience by claiming—as a new cardinal rule of witchcraft—that there was much greater magical power in old discarded things that were suddenly found to be just right for a certain witching job, than in any carefully constructed object.

"I mean," she pointed out to Jeannie, "it's what *real* magic is all about—things turning up in the right places at the right time."

So the plate was laid in the salad bowl (which only just accommodated it, strengthening Alison's theory that these things had been destined for each other). Then the salad bowl and plate were placed upon the table in the tower.

Now it must be admitted that at this stage of the arrangements Alison *had* tried a little harder than usual to go by the book. This had called for a covering of black material for the table, and since things had to be chalked or painted on it, around the Mirror, this seemed to make sense to her. Quickly discarding as too risky a first idea—of borrowing the only black garment she could think of, one of her mother's best nightdresses— she went on to consider swapping the green-topped table for the dark blue one after all. She even went down into the basement to re-examine the latter to make sure it was of a dark enough shade to pass for black in the shadowy tower.

"But it wasn't necessary," she declared proudly to Jeannie, puffing a little on her return. "Look what I found."

It was a small blackboard, not quite the size of the tabletop. It had been used for scoring at darts and other games in the playroom, and there was even a broken stick of chalk to go with it. Happily, they set to work cleaning the old markings off it with an especially strong solution of water and salt. Then, when it was barely dry, Alison inscribed upon it with chalk strokes as squeaky and sinister as her best witching voice, a large triangle: "The Triangle of Revelation," she explained to her sister.

The pedestal and Mirror were then placed inside the triangle, which had been turned with its point in the direction of the east (or what Alison fervently hoped was the east). Two of the candles, in a pair of candlesticks borrowed from the dining room, were placed one on either side of the triangle's point and lit. Then they were all set. Or almost.

"The page was torn out where it started to give you the incantations," said Alison. "But not to worry." She opened her Workbook. "I've made up some of my own. It should make the visions more *personal*."

Then, fully decked out in her poncho and Garter and Necklace, with the Workbook in her left hand and her Black-handled Knife in her right hand, held high in the air, like the Torch of Liberty, she high-stepped to the side of the table facing north and chanted:

> "Magic Mirror, deep and clear,
> Reveal your secrets to us here."

Next, with the candles flickering and stirring the shadows, she stepped to the side facing west:

> "Magic Mirror of power and mystery,
> Reveal the hidden ways of history."

Then on the side facing south:

> "Magic Mirror of love and hate,
> Bring us glimpses of our Fate."

Finally, with a flourish of the knife that nearly wafted
out the candles, Ariadne Atropos Arachne went to the
side facing east, at the blunt end of the triangle, and
intoned:

> "Magic Mirror, show us more
> Of what the future holds in store."

Jeannie, back in a corner behind her sister, was completely overawed—her eyes wide, her mouth open, her
hands clutching the notebook and pencil which Alison
had given her for the recording of visions as and when
they should be dictated by the seer. So overawed was
she, in fact, so entranced and enthralled, that she didn't
even think of asking for a turn at the Mirror herself
until, after about five minutes of stooping and frowning
into the blackened plate, Alison broke the silence and,
turning, said:

"Here, see if you can see anything. All I can see is
the candles flickering and my own reflection."

"Oh, yes, Ariadne!" whispered Jeannie, strictly correct
in her awe, and not in the least brought back to earth
by the everyday tone of her sister's voice. "Please! I'd
love to!"

With something of an indulgent sneer on her face, Alison took the book and pencil and stood aside.

"Well?"

Jeannie's stooping body seemed to stiffen almost at once, as she peered into the plate.

"I see . . . I think I see—" There was a puzzled note in Jeannie's whisper. "Yes, I do see—"

"What? The candles? Your—?"

"I see a little valley, yes . . . a little valley in the winter . . . covered in snow. . . ."

Alison craned forward suspiciously to get a better look at Jeannie's face. But her expression was quite serious, very intent.

"I see two little dark pools, side by side, in the snow. . . . I—I *think* they're pools. . . . They're dark and blurry at the edges. And—and oh!—in front of the pools . . . nearer this way . . ."

Alison felt her skin go prickly under the poncho.

"What?" she whispered. "Go on, Jea—er—Jezebel."

"Some snakes . . . two reddy-colored snakes—wriggling—I think they're fighting. . . ."

"Go on!"

Jeannie was silent for a while.

Then she shook her head.

"That's all," she sighed.

Her face was serious, still puzzled, slightly stunned. Alison had wondered for a moment if she might not have turned around grinning and saying something like: "Now it's only the commercials!" But then she remembered that if there was one thing her sister was *not*, it was a kidder.

"Would you—would you like to try again?" she asked. Jeannie blinked.

"Sure," she said. "I'll try."

This time her vision was more particular. It had Alison scribbling notes like mad at first, then tailing off in something like horror. . . .

"I see a tower, a tower like this one, only it is from the outside, and it is dark, and I am way, way down, looking up at it, and it's not on a house, it—it's just sticking out from the side of a mountain. And there's something else, something fluttering out of its windows, and I think, yes, it *is*—it's smoke, black smoke, getting thicker, and now there are flames, long licky flames, and oh!—golly!—there's someone in there—they're waving their arms out of the window, with the smoke and the flames. . . . And now . . . no . . . the smoke's too thick. . . . It's covering everything . . . it's all gone."

"Wow!" gasped Alison, in a most unwitchlike manner, as she stared at her sister. "I wonder . . ."

"You wonder what, Ariadne?" asked Jeannie, blinking at her dully.

"No . . . nothing. Er, just let me put these candles a little farther back. . . . That's better."

"Do you want me to see some more pictures?"

"Well—are you tired at all? I mean, do you *want* to?"

"Oh, sure."

Jeannie turned back with a strange kind of slow eagerness. Alison watched her stooping head with a new respect.

". . . a table . . ."

"A table? This table?"

". . . big table, long, with dishes with covers . . . White dishes on a white cloth. But now they're coming off, the covers . . . slowly. . . . And I see one dish is full of . . . brownies? . . . And another full of . . . stew? Oh, and here's one, a big one, with two midgets in it, alive, fighting, rocking the dish, making it go away in little jumps. . . . But here's another and—ooh!—a big fat speckled bird jumps out, onto the rim, and it is singing—I think—and its tongue has come out, a beautiful red and gold tongue, getting nearer, filling the Mirror, and the red and gold is in quarters, like a flag, and in one of the gold quarters there's a little picture of something, and now that quarter is getting nearer and I can see the picture and it's a cat, jumping up at something—yes, a black cat—and I think it's a fly it's trying to catch and—no, it's *not!*—it's a bird again, only a black bird this time. . . ."

At which point, according to the seer, the bird came so close that its wing blacked out the whole Mirror and then the vision was over.

Alison then knew just what comics meant on the television when they said: "How can you follow an act like *that?*"

Naturally, she tried very hard. She tried again and again. But mainly it was to see only the flickering candle flames and her own frowning eyes or pouching lips. Just once did she come anywhere near to having a vision, and even then it seemed to take shape away from the Mirror, as if she were seeing it out of her eye corners. This was a glimpse of a group of horses, white, brown, and black, with rich pink and blue saddles and harness, rearing up, giving trouble to a man who was holding them. There they reared and snorted, almost out of her field of vision, with olive-brown mountains and blackish trees behind them—a place that looked familiar, yet she felt sure she'd never been near it. And in front of the horses, closer to the Mirror, backs—men's backs, were they?—bending. . . . But then they faded.

"See anything, Ariadne?" asked Jeannie.

"Lots of things," said Alison sadly, "but too jumbled up to pick out."

That scrying session left Alison very thoughtful. Indeed, so impressed had she been by Jeannie's tower vision that she vowed never again to permit charcoal to be burned or candles to be lit up in *their* tower. What was more, she even began to wonder, gloomily, just who *was* the real witch in the family, she or the all-seeing Jeannie.

But then the sprightly green spirit of Ariadne M. seemed to clap her hands and tell her to snap out of it, and when bedtime came she was once more her old confident self.

"Jezebel," she said, sitting up in bed with a bounce, "the time has come for us to cast a spell."

"Mm . . ." Jeannie sounded drowsy. "What kind of spell?"

"A very special one."

Now Jeannie sat up, though rather more slowly. "Like making it rain, you mean?"

"Better. Much better. A really big one. And tomor-

row night's the night for it. A Tuesday. The new moon
. . . I've been looking it up."

"What does this spell do?"

"Well, it's really *part* of a spell—"

"Oh, just a part."

"But part of the Grand Bewitchment—the part where
the Devil Is Raised."

"Eh? The—the *Devil?* Oh, Alison, are you sure—"

"Sure, I'm sure! The power that we can pack between
us, why, we'll have him dancing for us up in the tower
like that bear in the circus last year!"

"No! I mean is it *safe?*"

"Of course it's safe. It tells you all the proper pre-
cautions in the book."

CHAPTER 11

Raising the Devil

Now you must know (as the Witch Book author was forever saying) —you must know that the Grand Bewitchment spell, of which the Devil Raising is such an important part, is the most complicated and difficult of them all. It is without doubt the Big One—to be tackled only by the most intrepid and skilled of adepts. Indeed, it had only been included in *The Secret Arts of Witchcraft* as a kind of showpiece—to let the beginners see just how tough it could be at the top.

But we already know that Ariadne Atropos Arachne was the most slapdash, headlong, corner-cutting, overhasty, harum-scarum, hit-or-miss, slaphappy, trigger-happy, breakneck, hell-bent, hotfooted, bull-rushing Beginner Witch ever to trip over a broomstick. A caster of spells? A *hurler* of them, all bundled up, hugger-mugger and higgledy-piggledy, was what *this* witch was.

So:

Where the book called for the Chalice to be filled with bitter wine (myrrh), she filled it with half a can of her father's beer (Milwaukee's finest).

Where the book insisted upon a mixture of something called "graveyard dust," black poppy seeds, bitter aloes, hawthorn blossoms, pulverized juniper wood (with berries), henbane, jimsonweed, and hemlock (to mention only a few of the ingredients), she provided a mess of dead flies entangled in a spider web and half a pack of mixed herbs that she managed to rustle up from the kitchen.

The book was very precise about calculations connected with the spell. It had to be a Tuesday, at midnight, just before the new moon. Well, it *was* a Tuesday, and even if it wasn't exactly *before* a new moon, it was only a night or two after. As for the midnight bit, again there were problems. (Mainly the fact that if the sorceresses waited for midnight they'd be sure to fall asleep.) So Alison timed it for ten, and she consoled herself and her Deputy with the thought that it was certain to be midnight *somewhere*, in some other time zone, so what difference would it make to the Devil?

But the book was not only precise in its time calculations; it was also very strict about directions and distances and quantities. Lining the table up with its triangle pointing north caused no trouble, of course. But to insist on having the whole thing enclosed in a chalked or painted nine-foot-diameter magic circle in a room that was only six feet at it widest—that was just plain stupid, decided Alison. And she promptly made hers five.

As for the procedure: chaos.

There was the grinding of the herbs and graveyard dust, with incantations, clearly stipulated by the book as something to be done with a mortar and pestle. Ariadne

Atropos Arachne simply shook them up in the coffee jar she'd brought them in, considering them to be finely ground enough already.

There was the mixing of this mess with beeswax. She used some modeling clay bought from the village store.

The gritty clay was then supposed to be fashioned into the shape of the victim you wished the Devil to go and lean on, once raised. Since they were skipping the victim bit and merely bringing the Horned One up for a social visit, they made it a model of himself— and very fine he looked too, with horns that were so big he kept toppling forward on his face, and Deputy Jezebel had to be reprimanded for laughing.

Engraving the victim's name on the model with the tip of the knife was out in this version of course, but who was worried? THE DEVIL—that was the inscription that Ariadne Atropos Arachne scrawled on his backside (which had to be enlarged to get the last IL on comfortably).

A dab of wine (beer on this occasion) was then placed between the horns as she intoned the modified chant:

> "In the name of the Horned One,
> Creature of wax I name thee The Devil."

Which was pretty much the same as naming the guy in the name of the guy—but again, who cared?

Then there was a great deal of fussing about which hand you held the puppet in while you tapped and stroked life into it with the Wand. (This witch had a thing about using the Knife instead of a Wand—not because it would have been too difficult to make one, especially now that she was mobile again, but—well—because it felt more like *her*.) And then, with the puppet placed in the Altar Triangle, head to the north (though even that was bungled, in a way, with one of the horns, too heavily tapped by the Wand, bending due west), there was a lot of intricate byplay with the Red Candle of Bewitchment. To give her her due, Alison followed this last quite faithfully—save that she'd substituted a red-cased flashlight for the candle, on account of her sister's disturbing vision in the Mirror.

And then—

But why go on?

As far as the book was concerned, the end result of all the recommended detailed care and caution, the exactitude and pinpoint specification, was the Raising of the Devil.

Whereas the end result of all *their* slap and dash, all *their* approximations and substitutions, that night, up in the tower, was the Raising of—

"*Daddy!*"

During the two or three seconds before Jeannie's scream, there had been a petrified silence.

The girls had been *expecting* the Devil, remember. No matter how fully or faintly, they had been expecting some sort of apparition, be it only a thickening of the shadows, with a shaping of that thickening into some semblance of horns around the head, and perhaps, as a bonus, with a tail-like tapering trailing behind.

And what they saw, in the shadows, with the creak of the door and the gasp of the visitor, was this bulky

man-shape, stooping, glass gleaming brightly in his eyes.
The dusty smudges on his cheek and forehead, collected
on his dark and unfamiliar journey through closet and
cistern room, looked like smears of soot from hell; and
there was on his head a crownlike wreath of webs, tangled
in his hair, giving an impression of madness and ragged
abandon almost as macabre as horns.

As for Mr. McNair—after noticing from the driveway
the flickering lights in the slits of the tower, and investigating the girls' bedroom and finding their beds
empty—he'd naturally expected to find his daughters in
that tower. You didn't have to be a detective for *that*,
he'd told himself grimly, as he'd edged and stooped and
bumped his way past pipes and tank toward the chant-
ings and mumblings. But what he wasn't prepared for
was the sight of them like that: the bulbs around their
necks, barefooted, in loose dark robes of some kind,
with a knife held high, and all of it—all of this wildness
—permeated by a strong smell of *beer!*

"What in—!" he growled, stepping forward and grabbing the goblet. He took a quick sniff, then a sip.
"Yes—*beer!*" he cried. "What *is* all this?"

"Well, we didn't come here to drink it, if that's what
you're thinking," said Alison, with a shrug of disgust at
the ruining of their spell.

"Oh no, Daddy!" said Jeannie, overbrimming with
friendliness in her vast relief. "That was just to put
between his eyes."

"*His?* Whose?"

"The Devil's, Daddy. You see, we're playing at witches
and—"

"We were *not*—" Alison was going to say that they were be no means *playing* at it, then thought better of it. Their father was smiling, which was at least something to be thankful for.

"A fine game for this time of night," he said, still grinning. "Then you wonder why you have nightmares. . . ." He turned to Alison. "I suppose this was your idea, young lady?"

She shrugged again, acting once more on her theory that the less one said and did in such circumstances, the sooner it would be forgotten. But Jeannie's tongue was still tingling with the shock, eager to wag and twitch and curl and flicker.

"Yes, but some of it was mine, Daddy, and I can see better than her in the Magic Mirror—would you like me to show you? And one day soon we'll be able to make it rain—won't we, Ariadne?—that's her Witch Name, she has three, and mine's *Jezebel*, and—"

"Ariadne and Jezebel, eh?" Their father's voice was trembling, the eyes behind the glasses sparkling. *Oh, great!* thought Ariadne Atropos Arachne. *Oh, what a fun topic the next time there was a party—these two kids of mine, wouldja believe—witches! No kidding! Up there in the tower, all geared up!* "Well, Ariadne, Jezebel, I guess —" *A crack about broomsticks*, thought Alison. *I can smell it coming, you don't need the Pendulum for that. And, yes, there!* "—you'd better climb aboard your broomsticks and take off for Dreamland."

As they made their way out, past the pipes in the cistern room and the cases in the closet, Alison said, with her best COLD expression (upper lip long, lower lip tight, eyes fixed on a speck an immense distance away in an imaginary firmament):

"Broomsticks are just part of the *popular* idea of witchcraft. It's not like that at all."

But this only made her father laugh louder than ever, and she wished she'd maintained a disdainful silence.

"As for you," she muttered to her sister, a few minutes later, when they'd been seen into their beds and the light was switched off, "you ought to be—"

A babble of voices, laced with laughter like the froth on beer, rose from below, making her break off and groan.

"Yes, Alison?"

"I've a good mind to fire you. Spilling it all like that."

"Oh, well . . ."

"Never mind 'Oh, well'! You know what'll happen *now*, don't you?"

"You—you mean they'll not let us play witches again?"

"'*Play*'!" Alison gritted her teeth. "Oh, sure, they'll let us *play* witches all right!"

"Well—that's all right then. Isn't it?"

"Of course it's not all right. Not when you're a real witch, a serious witch, a—a *pro* witch—like me."

"But—"

"It destroys all the secrecy. They—they'll be watching everything we do from now on."

"But—if they think we're only *playing* . . ."

Not for the first time, Alison felt herself being pulled up short by something in her sister. It could hardly be called *sense*. And yet . . .

"Oh, well, maybe you're right," she said. "But it's

not going to be easy anymore, all the stupid cracks *they'll* be making."

"What cracks?"

"You heard *him* just now, didn't you? We'll be getting that from all of them—you'll see. Broomsticks for breakfast, broomsticks for lunch, broomsticks for supper. It's going to be *sick-making!*"

At that there was a long silence. Then:

"Alison . . ."

"Yes. What is it this time?"

"All the cracks they'll be making . . ."

"What about them?"

"Well, it's better than being burned, like the old witches."

"Huh!"

"And Alison . . ."

"What?"

"Can't we put a spell on them all, make them all forget they ever found out about us being witches?"

Oh, to be a simple child again! thought Alison. One minute they think they're playing at witches and the next they're seriously proposing a tongue-binding spell of the greatest complexity. That's what the book said. "Of the greatest complexity."

In the darkness, she put on the PATIENT face, said: "We'll see!"—and turned over to the wall.

CHAPTER 12

Persecution

Alison was right. The family may not have harped on broomsticks quite as much as she'd predicted, but they certainly had their fill of fun at the girls' expense.

Even their mother joined in: at first asking such things as did they have a special powder to slip into the golf bag of her closest rival and fellow beginner, Mrs. Swarthout—something that would cause that lady to slice every stroke she made. Then, when *that* big joke —that "big, big, screamingly funny joke," as Alison, muttering, kept calling it—was played out, Mrs. McNair began modifying her cracks in a typically sneaky motherly way, saying things like:

"Come on, Jezebel, eat up your carrots, dear, they'll make you see better in the dark."

Or:

"A real witch wouldn't be so anxious to get back to the city, Ariadne. You should be very happy in the country, what with all these spooky trees and owls and toads, and all."

Their father was equally obnoxious. Every morning, when he came down to breakfast, and every evening, after a spell away from the house, he would greet them with:

"How are my two little witches?"

Day after day after day he kept this up, until it became like an incantation in itself, guaranteed to do the thoroughly witchlike job of conjuring demons of fury in the elder of those "two little witches." As for his remarks at parties and to strangers or visitors, again it was just as Alison had foreseen: everyone he talked to had to be told the story of his trip to the tower and the sight that had met him there. In fact, she didn't know what infuriated her more: his straight repetition of the same old basic story or his additions and amendments, made usually during the parties, after a few drinks.

"I mean, I wouldn't *mind*," she confided in Jeannie, "if he'd just stick to the truth. But some nights it's wine, not beer, we were supposed to have had in the Chalice, and other nights it's whiskey. And how anyone can laugh so much at his own story, after telling it for the three millionth time, I just don't know."

Mr. McNair even went so far as to bring it up with Mr. Crowther one afternoon, just as they were all going out in the car and the gardener happened to walk past. Admittedly, the man was carrying his broom, so that the comment must have been irresistible. At any rate, Alison saw it coming. She groaned softly, rolling up her eyes even as her father chuckled noisily and rolled down his window.

"Better keep an eye on *that*, Rick!"

Mr. Crowther came to a stop, slowly turning his head. He'd obviously been deep in thought, probably working out his latest move in his war with the game warden of his muttered reflections.

"Huh?"

"That broomstick, Rick . . ."

The man was now quite still, staring at Mr. McNair, stooping slightly, his head to one side. Only his eyes moved, glittering from face to face. The broom itself might have been part of him, its stick the same pale earthy color as the hand that held it, with similar curves and lumps.

"What about it?"

"I said you'd better keep an eye on it. We have two witches here."

For a moment a gleam of terror slid across the glittering eyes, steadying them. Then he looked down, almost shyly, and flicked the bristles across his boots.

"It don't do to be making jokes like that," he mumbled. "No, sir. Not about witches. Not about him, not where he's concerned, this one."

With a thrill, Alison realized he was talking about the broom as if it were a living being. She nudged Jeannie, who was sitting with her on the back seat, and nodded toward their father's face—off which the gardener's strange remark had swept the smile as surely as if by the bristles of the broom itself.

"Huh?" Now it was Mr. McNair's turn to grunt and gape like a peasant, and it was a delightful thing to behold. "I—er—you talking about the broom?"

"Yes, *sir*. Yes, sir, he *is* bewitched, this one. Yes, sir. Oh, yes indeedy. I could tell you tales about this one, eh, ya varmint?" Here Mr. Crowther gave the broom a vi-

cious sideways kick, causing it to leap and twirl yet still
not leave his hand. "He's got a mean sense o' humor
when the mood's on him. Yes, sir. Likes to roam around
the shed there, one place to another. Likes to fool me being where he wasn't put when I went out when I get back.
Likes to *try*," the Grouch added darkly, peering into the
back of the car and nodding hard.

Not once did he show by so much as a wink or a
twitch or a flicker that he was referring to the afternoon
of Alison's foray into the shed. Yet her breath came
quicker—just as it had when she'd been making that and
other excursions into the world of witchery.

And it surely cast a spell on her father—the gardener's
reaction to his joking. For the rest of the afternoon Mr.
McNair was very subdued, shake his head as much as he
might and give as his opinion that Mr. Crowther was a
little—well—not quite sound in his mind. Why, it was at
least twenty-four hours before he made his "How are my
two little witches?" remark again—and in Alison's esti-
mation the dour gardener went up twenty points or more.

"You'd better believe it," she told Jeannie later. "Old
Grouch, old *Mister* Grouch, is one of the sanest, wisest
—most *sagacious*—people around this place. I only hope
he's friendly, that's all. I know I wouldn't like to be that
game warden he keeps muttering about. . . ."

But this was only one bright patch in a very irritating,
uncomfortable, unlucky period. The inane cracks continued, with brother Tom's being too stupid to think
about, let alone repeat—so stupid in fact that he had finally to be pulled up sharply in one of his repeated
requests for the young witches to "make up a love

potion, huh, to slip into Sharon Cranshaw's Coke next time I see her."

"All right," said Alison one day, after days of ignoring this question with her best BORED expression. "All right, Tom," she said, enlivening her features with her sharpest EAGER look. "I haven't answered this request before because the moon hasn't been right, but yes, sure. We'll mix a love potion for Sharon. There's the most powerful of all, with motherwort in it, and violet petals, and a touch of verbena, and a sprinkling of periwinkle dust. We'll use that. Next time she comes visiting or—oh, maybe at a party or a cookout . . . Anyway, just leave it to us."

"Hey, now, wait a minute, Sis," said Tom at that. "I was only fooling."

"Ah, but I was not!" said Alison, in her creakiest voice. "Were we, sister?" she added, giving Jeannie a nudge.

"Yeah, but wait!" gasped Tom. "I mean—you really know how? I mean, you have a recipe and all?"

"Sure!" said Jeannie, catching on.

"Of a certainty," said Alison, striving for a more sinister note and nodding sagely.

"Yeah, but—no—gee! You might poison her!"

"That," said Ariadne Atropos Arachne, with veiled eyes, "is something that has to be risked."

"Hey, but no! Forget it. Forget I asked."

"Too late, too late," sighed Ariadne, eyes almost closed now. "The order has gone in. . . ."

And no matter how he pleaded with them, or promised to drop the ribbing, the witches refused to budge, saying that in all good time, maybe when he'd forgotten, the potion would surely be compounded and the philter slipped, all unsuspected, into the drink of his heart's desire.

"Well, that was another bright spot, I guess," Alison wrote in a letter to Emmeline, toward the end of the vacation. Then she remembered their code and continued as follows:

> But this is really to three to four to tell you vee you double-you that I'm so looking forward threeward twoward seeing you soon and making baking shaking you my partner in witch- in who- in what- in witchcraft. Jeannie's all right all left all brought, but she soon gets tired gets wheeled gets braked and wants to play with her dolls. I mean, for the five the six the last three weeks she's hardly softly loudly given it a thought a speech a song, but I swear unto you this: that before befive besix we leave we twig we branch we limb this place, she shall witness a real a rod a line a hook a spell, and it is one is two is three that I have been preparing preorangeing preappleing very carefully brimmingly spillingly.

It was a code not likely to cause overwhelming difficulties to an expert government-agency full-time professional cipher-breaker, of course. But then, Alison and Emmeline had no intention of ever trying to baffle any expert government-agency full-time professional cipher-breakers. At one time, very early in their code-concocting careers, they might have entertained the shadow of such a hope; but it wasn't long before they realized that such

a standard meant hours and hours of hard, painfully boring work to produce the simplest of messages—and in
circumstances of that sort Emmeline was just as impatient as Alison.

No, all they wished to defeat were the prying eyes of
curious parents or brothers or sisters, into whose hands
there was always a possibility that a message might fall—
the sort of amateur who would like to know what was
being communicated, but who wouldn't be anxious
enough to go to much trouble to dig for a meaning.

"So if we keep putting in extra words it'll look like
nonsense—it won't even look like a code," Alison had
said.

"Yes, but . . ." Emmeline's round placid face had
creased up a little here. "How will *we* be able to make
sense of it?"

"Easy. I've given this a lot of thought. We simply stick
in words every so often. Words that sound like or look
like or have the same meaning as or are the opposites of
the last true word to be written. You'll soon get the
hang the bang the dangle the drape of it."

"Eh?"

"That was just an example. I meant you'll soon get
the hang of it."

"Oh . . ." Emmeline's blank face had suddenly split
into a smile. "I think I see I lake I ocean what you
mean."

Simple, then, and if it wasn't quite as baffling as they'd
hoped, even for their very humble purposes, it was
certainly more fun to write than the usual substitution
of figures for letters would have been. However, it did

tend to take up a lot of space—so, after shaking all the
extra code words out of it, this is how Alison's letter
continued:

> I will not say what the spell will be exactly, except
> two things. Item 1. It is a *benevolent* kind of spell,
> which is where we went wrong with the Devil Rais-
> ing one, I guess, on account that we are good-doing
> witches with no business with the Devil AT ALL,
> though I swear to you, Emmeline, we did not figure
> on using him to do bad things for us, just to look at
> him and see what he looks like. O.K. Item 2. We
> have found another place for a den after the tower
> was so cruelly desecrated by the intrusion of an Un-
> believer, our very witty Father. This place . . .

Here even Alison's plain uncoded text became a little
complicated and rambling, as a result of her not being
really sure whether she should be divulging this, even
to her best friend and future witching partner. But
eventually she decided it could do no harm, and she
disclosed such facts as that it was an old summerhouse,
with peeling paint, close to the woods in a corner of its
own, nearly surrounded by shrubbery.

> Its door is off its hinges and all its windows are
> out and it is even dirtier than the tower, with not
> only webs and dust but bird droppings all over the
> seats around its sides like the shelf in the tower. I
> mean, the seats are just bench-type, sticking out
> like the shelf in the tower, not that the shelf in
> the tower had bird droppings on it, it didn't. The
> Grouch said it was built by an Englishman who

owned the place thirty years ago because it reminded him of his home in somewhere called Slop-
shire or something like that. I knew what he meant,
he meant his English home had a summerhouse
just like that, but I pretended not to understand
and I said to Grouch what a funny little house it
must have been to be as small as this old summerhouse, and Grouch got grouchier and said: "There
was nothing to laugh at about old Mr. Maltravers
and his summerhouse because the poor old man died
in this very summerhouse one hot afternoon with a
heart attack and his body wasn't found until late at
night." Of course I had no idea and I said I was sorry
for laughing, but as I turned away there was a
thoughtful gleam in Ariadne Atropos Arachne's eyes,
for all at once it had come to her what a wonderful
place for a new den this would be, with a history
like that, and especially for the spell I had in mind,
which was . . .

Here Alison had undergone an agony of indecision,
continuing after much thought with:

Oh Emmeline, ought I tell you? I do not see
why not, but I do not want to spoil the chances
of this spell, yet then again maybe I ought to tell
someone in case something goes wrong and Jezebel
and I suffer the fate of Mr. Maltravers and get
found dead in there and maybe poor old Grouch
gets the blame and spends the rest of his life in jail,
which would kill him without his broom and his
mower and his other tools, and grouch though he

is, I could not let that happen. So, Emmeline, in greatest secrecy, just in case we are found dead and an innocent person is accused, just so you can clear his name, here is the spell we are preparing to cast just before we return to New York. It is . . .

And at this point the writer really poured the code on thick—so thick and fruity that it deserves quoting in full:

It is called is named is addressed the Dumb the dam the dim the dome the doom Supper sup him sup them sip this, and it is the spell the write the wrote that raises lifts heaves elevates the shade sunglasses blind of a loved one two three four who has fairly lightly softly gently recently renickelly redimely redollarly died.

Which, translated by Emmeline, not without many a false step (such as trying to visualize a ghost in sunglasses) and much hard thinking and a final shiver, read:

It is called the Dumb Supper, and it is the spell that raises the shade of a loved one who has fairly recently died.

After which the letter needed no translation, being written, on account of the lateness of the hour and the excitement of the writer (now that the main disclosure had been made), in plain text, thus:

We thought of Mr. Maltravers first, since after all he did die in there, but of course he was not one of our loved ones even if he might have been the Grouch's, and besides it is best if it is recent and that was 30 years ago (tho' to a witch even 30 years

is but a minute, I guess) . Anyway, the best loved
one we knew who died most recently was poor dear
Norton who was hit by a taxi on Madison Avenue
where he would keep straying after that lady Siamese
in the art dealer's on the opposite corner, as you
know, dear Emmeline. And it is he who we shall
raise the shade of on the Thursday before the
Monday we return home.

CHAPTER 13

The Dumb Supper

Important though the new spell was—especially as Alison tried so hard to stick to the instructions this time (with certain unavoidable differences and unquestionable improvements)—it is necessary first to describe Norton. After all, his was the shade that the two sisters hoped to conjure in this last desperate bid to prove the potency of their witchhood.

Here then are the facts about the subject:

> Feline. Male. Age 4 when killed. Black (with white star under chin and one white paw, left rear). Eyes: green. Disposition: affectionate (particularly toward Alison, Jeannie, and the lady Siamese at the art dealer's on Madison). Health: good. Appetite: excellent. Intelligence: quite high, except when distracted by thoughts of aforementioned Siamese. Peculiarities: 1. his call or cry or greeting, always a quiet single "Purrup!" 2. his habit of jumping, with wide inquiring eyes, onto the lap or sometimes the shoulder of anyone who sneezed.

And now the facts about the spell that was being prepared in the hope of bringing him back, at least in spirit, however fleetingly—the renowned act of white magic known to witches everywhere as The Dumb Supper.

Its purpose (wrote the author of *The Secret Arts of Witchcraft*) *is the wholly benevolent one of evoking from the abyss of Death the shade of someone dearly loved. It calls for careful preparation over a period of thirteen days, culminating in a ritual meal, of which the loved one is invited to partake. The food and drink provided should of course be those which were the departed one's favorites in life. . . .*

Leaving the details of the preparations and ritual aside for the moment, it cannot be too firmly stressed that the key to the whole operation was this question of the choice of menu. The author of the book, not having the shades of animals in mind, failed, understandably, to clear up a matter that looked as if it would capsize the whole enterprise from the very beginning. She had taken it for granted that the workers of the spell wouldn't mind joining the loved one in his repast, whether it happened to be their favorite food or not. But Jezebel/Jeannie had other ideas.

"Well, I don't mind drinking milk out of a saucer, but I'm *not* going to eat Kittychow, not even a spoonful!"

And it has to be admitted that Ariadne/Alison had somewhat the same views, even though she would have been game, on a pinch, for eating just a crumb or two of the canned food.

However, as usual, her nimble imagination and fierce high seriousness came to the rescue.

"We-e-ll . . . it doesn't say *straight out* that we have to eat the same things as the loved one," she murmured, poring over the book. "I mean it—whatdyoucallit?—it—it *implies* that we should, but it doesn't say it straight out."

Whereupon she frowned deeply for a second or two, then shrugged and, shutting the book with a snap and a suddenly clear face, said:

"That settles it then. Norton can have Kittychow and milk, and we'll have milk and Hershey bars."

And so, on the appointed day, at about twenty minutes to the appointed hour (of noon), the two girls walked casually down the garden with strange looks on their faces (pinched, wary, but bright of eye) and strange lumps under their shirts.

Alison's was the larger, since she was carrying the can of cat food and the carton of milk; but Jeannie's was the more peculiar, since its shape kept shifting around and changing and causing her now to wince and now to giggle softly in thin explosions through her nose. This was because it was composed of smooth, slippery things like saucers, and prickly things like the can opener and the stiff wrapper ends of the candy bars.

"Be quiet!" warned Alison as they approached the shrubbery that screened the summerhouse. "And for heaven's sakes hold yourself looser and look more casual."

Jeannie's idea of looking loose and casual was to act as if she were on the point of throwing up. But she had to put her arms around her stomach like that to make sure her share of the equipment didn't fall out of her shirt when she made her legs go floppy. So Alison forgave her and concentrated instead on looking back at the house.

It was horned and brooding under a thunderously blackening sky, as if it knew what they were about, and was jealous of the summerhouse, and wishing them all kinds of bad luck in their project. But it was deserted just then, and that was all that mattered. So was the garden—what she could see of it—with the puttering of Mr. Crowther's mower reassuring her that he was somewhere on the other side of the house.

"Right," said Alison, turning to her accomplice. "From now on, absolute silence and all walking to be done backwards. . . ."

Which was how they covered the last thirty feet or so along the path through the shrubs.

As has been mentioned already, they had observed with the utmost care all the preliminaries laid down in the book, switching only where it had been absolutely unavoidable, or where an obvious improvement—fully in tune with the spirit of the operation—had presented itself.

Thus there was the problem of timing the rite for midnight. This would have meant not just the one nocturnal visit to the summerhouse, but thirteen preparatory trips at the same hour—a luck-pushing schedule far too risky to contemplate, quite apart from Alison's earlier objections to midnight as being too late and too likely to find them fast asleep.

"But why not mid*day*?" she had said eventually. "I mean, that's just as special a time as midnight—as, as *potent*—isn't it?"

"Yes, or *dawn*. How about dawn?" Jeannie had asked, with one of her flashes of occult intelligence. "That's when they used to make sacrifices, those old tribes in—"

"Yes, yes!" Alison had interrupted quickly, foreseeing difficulties here almost as great as the midnight ones. "But midday will do. After all, we are *good* witches, *day* witches, and that's just got to be our witching hour. And besides"—this was added in a more subdued, sadder, sighing tone—"it's nearer the time of day when poor Norton got killed."

This had also been why she had chosen a Thursday. The book had suggested some anniversary as being the best time for the rite, but since Norton had been dead for only four months or so, Alison had had to make do with the mere day of the week. Now that they'd decided to make it nearer the actual time of that day, she felt better.

So, for thirteen days, the two sisters had found excuses for visiting the summerhouse around noon, there to set up a shrine on the bench along the west wall. This shrine—the materials for which they had secreted, along with their Necklaces, the Black-handled Knife, the Workbook, and other paraphernalia of their craft, under a loose floorboard in a dark corner—was quite simple. The centerpiece was an old, faded, dog-eared (or, as Alison preferred to think of it, being nothing if not consistent, *cat*-eared) snapshot of Norton himself, huge of eye and bristly of neck, as he stared up at the flash-

bulb glare from his corner of the couch. This picture was propped up against the wall after being veiled in the darkest cloth they could find, a blue silk handkerchief they'd borrowed from Tom's room. And then, on either side of this, they placed small bunches of wild flowers which they replenished when they began to fade and wither: some daisies, as a rule, or sprays of goldenrod, or butterfly weed. Entwined with these there would always be a sprig or two of catnip from a clump that Alison had been delighted to find in the front garden.

On these preliminary visits, the procedure would be the same each time. Jeannie would stand guard at the door while Alison, wearing her Necklace, would fix the red flashlight on the bench opposite, so that its pale beam was trained on the darkly veiled snapshot. Then she would sprinkle over the shrine fragments of rubbed and shredded catnip leaf (which was her choice instead of burning incense as the book asked), after which she would sit on the floor, facing the photograph, with the flashlight behind her, calling softly, "Norton, Norton, Nortie, Nortie, Norton!" as she thought of happy incidents involving the cat. Sometimes she thought so vividly of these things that tears would come to her eyes.

According to the book, this thirteen-day warming-up period was to alert the spirit of the dead loved one to what was being planned—a kind of ghostly party invitation—and to get it all tuned up for putting in an appearance at the appointed time. *Well*—Alison had thought, brushing the tears away after the final run-through—*if he won't come up for his party after all this, it'll be because he's found someone's departed Siamese down there. . . .*

Alison was thinking of all these preparations as she walked backwards into the summerhouse that final Thursday. With every step of the last thirty feet or so, the sky seemed to have grown darker until now—on the threshold of her Venture into the Unknown (as she described it to herself)—it was almost as dark as the originally prescribed midnight hour itself.

It was fitting, she thought, gazing around and gently putting out a hand to bring her backwards-walking Deputy to a halt. If magical deeds were ever to be accomplished at all—which they must—then this was the atmosphere for them. Even Jeannie seemed to be feeling the same. No silly gasp had escaped her when, on being checked by Alison's hand, a rattle of thunder had rolled around their heads. All was solemn, solemn. . . .

Swiftly, silently, steady with all those days of practice, they prepared the final ritual. While Alison put on her Necklace and Garter and set up the shrine, Jeannie spread a napkin on the floor in the middle of the room and set down four saucers on the pale square: two close together on the side nearest the shrine, the other two opposite.

Then, when Alison had switched on the flashlight and sprinkled catnip on the shrine, she went to help her sister. Into one of the saucers nearest the shrine went some of the milk, and large succulent chunks of cat food were tumbled into its companion. A strong, quite appetizing smell went up as this was done, and as Jeannie sniffed appreciatively she seemed about to say something. A fierce warning frown from Alison checked her.

Then milk was poured into the other two saucers, and a candy bar set down at the side of each. After this, they both sat silent, cross-legged, Jeannie staring at her Hershey bar, Alison gazing at her watch.

As soon as the second hand indicated that it was midday precisely, Alison stood up, turned, sidestepped, and began to approach the shrine backwards, very slowly. It had to be slow because, between meal and photograph, she had to repeat silently certain lines of verse, and there were four of them, and the room was so small.

These lines she had made up herself. She'd had to, since the book's incantation had been designed strictly for the souls of humans, not cats. And these lines were:

By the powers that bind all cats
To work with witches to the last,
I call thee now to come to us,
Spirit of Norton, our dear puss.

With the last word of the last line, she felt the edge
of the bench against the back of her right knee, and she
jumped slightly for it felt just like the discreet tap that
Norton sometimes gave you with his paw when he was
lying on a chair and feared you might be going to sit
on him.

She stood stock-still, her mouth dry, listening. Through
the glassless windows came a sudden rustling of leaves,
as if the first gust of the storm had arrived. But this
was not so, because after the rustling came the perfect
calm-before-storm silence again, no longer broken even
by Mr. Crowther's mower motor. She began to wonder
where the man was, then stopped, telling herself to
concentrate. The most crucial part of the ritual was just
about to take place.

Turning at right angles to the bench, the side of her
right leg against its edge, she retreated, walking backwards again, but in a circular, clockwise direction that
took her all around the saucers once and then back
next to her sister, where she sat down again.

Together they drank from their saucers, Alison hoping
that Jeannie would remember that she mustn't on any
account look at the veiled snapshot. Then they unwrapped
their candy bars and ate them, swiftly, steadily, solemnly,
still not looking toward the shrine.

When they were through, Alison touched her sister's
arm warningly and got up again. This time she walked

backwards to the flashlight and turned it off. Then, turning, she walked backwards to her place, turned again, sat, and touched her sister again.

Whereupon they both closed their eyes, as arranged and practiced, and broke the silence together, calling, softly but insistently, in unison:

"Norton! Norton! Norton!"

To Alison the dimness of the summerhouse seemed to go dimmer still, as far as she could tell through her tightly closed eyelids.

Then she heard a rustle again, from outside.

Followed by—a *scratching* noise?

She felt her sister jump as a light clump followed the scratching. She wondered for a moment if it had been Jeannie who'd been making those sounds.

But is *was* only for a moment.

For in the very next instant came a plaintive bleat —half wail, half howl—and a cry of "Yeeow!"

And then she just had to open her eyes to see what had made it.

Clinging together in a rapt and terrified—but so deliciously, so triumphantly terrified—silence, the two girls stared at their guest.

It was a cat, yes, but not a black cat.

This one was gray, blue-gray all over, and it seemed only half grown, still in the late stages of kittenhood.

But at least two of its paws were white, including the left rear one, and there was no doubt about its liking for Kittychow as, shoulders hunched, ruff bristling, whiskers working, it drove its nose into the chunks of meat, plowing a slow broad furrow through them. Neither was there any doubt about the one eye that they could see, warily cocked at them. Even in the dimness the green shone bright and clear, a true Norton traffic-light green if ever there was one.

In silence and wonder they watched the cat demolish the meat, and turn to the milk, and sniff, and lap it all up with a loud, wet, unbroken rhythm, and then return to the meat saucer and snuffle out the spilled crumbs from under the rim. Then, after it had lifted its head and given a final glance around, it made a slight half-conscious pawing, scratching movement on the napkin, and Jeannie could no longer contain herself.

"That's just what Norton used to do!" she cried.

The cat crouched in alarm and made a faint hissing noise.

"So is that!" said Alison. "In fact, that cat *is* Norton, it just has to be . . . hasn't it, honey?" she crooned, swooping and picking it up in her arms and holding it close to her chest.

It gave her bulb-necklace a halfhearted dab, then went soft and relaxed and purred so loud it seemed fit to give itself a sore throat.

The first drops of rain had started to fall as the two girls ran crowing and squealing with delight up the path to the house.

Mr. Crowther paused at the door of his shed and watched them come.

"Mr. Crowther, Mr. Crowther, look! Look what *we've* got!" cried Jeannie, running alongside her sister with a hand gently but firmly fixed on the newcomer's head, where it was still resting against the Necklace.

"Huh! So that's where *they* got to, is it?" growled the gardener, staring at the string of bulbs.

"No, she means the cat!" said Alison, all grins, not in the least worried about being found out, not worried about anything at all now, thunder or lightning or the wrath of gardeners, even gardeners with brooms in their hands and secrets of their own lurking deep in their eyes.

"Oh, that!" The Grouch bunched up his mouth, making a million raylike wrinkles appear at the edges. "Some stray, huh?"

"No, no!" said Jeannie. "It's ours. He got run over by a taxi four months ago, and now he's come back to life."

Mr. Crowther scowled with surprise and sympathy.

"Well I'll be darned!" he said. And: "How about that, ya dog?" he added, still staring at the cat but kicking the broomstick, which leapt and twirled in his hand again.

There was absolutely no glimmer of recognition in his eyes though, nor the faintest flicker of a twinkle there. Just this strange dull mixture of surprise and sympathy. Alison remembered it clearly, hours later, and it made their parents' theory (that the kitten had been brought by Mr. Crowther from a home that didn't want it and craftily planted on them) sound all the more ridiculous.

No, thought Alison that night in bed, with the cat soundly sleeping across her feet in true Familiar fashion, *there's no doubt about where* he *came from.*

And so she fell asleep—content, supremely confident again, fulfilled, equipped—all set for her return to New York and what was to be (though she did not know it yet) her last great work of witchery.

CHAPTER 14

The Magical Attack

"I tell you we're under attack!"

Alison turned from the window of her room and glared at her companions. Behind her, the lights in the windows of the apartments opposite were beginning to take on deeper but brighter shades of lemon or pink, while the narrow column of sky between the new building opposite and the older one on the right was now quite violet higher up—a column of deepening violet between soft, rough, dried-blood red and the gray of ghosts, of decaying, peeling toadstools.

"A heavy attack," she added. "From somewhere over there."

A siren's thin scream cut through the throbbing violet and the rush of traffic.

"A heavy *magical* attack," she said, as if to dissociate it from the noisy perils of the city.

"Why out there?" asked Jeannie, who was sitting on the bed and nursing the gray cat, which—after much begging and pleading and the threat of a hunger strike—they'd been allowed to bring home with them. "I should think it's Old Grouch. I mean, you say yourself he's a male witch."

"Not from *that* distance," said Alison. "And anyway, something tells me he's always been on our side. He wouldn't do a thing like this."

"I'm still not sure what you mean," said Emmeline Grant, looking at them through the reflection in the dressing-table mirror, where she'd been trying on Alison's poncho. "What exactly *is* a magical attack?"

"It's when another—"

"Be quiet!" snapped Alison to Jeannie. "Remember what I said. We're only allowing you in here with us if you don't interrupt, don't get in the way, and don't blabber anything we say to anybody else. Right?"

"Well, I've been a witch longer than her, even if she is older and—"

"Jeannie . . ."

Jeannie quailed under Alison's stern scowl, then sighed with such an exaggerated heaving of the shoulders that the cat got up and jumped off her lap.

"There!" said Alison. "Even Norton knows when you're stepping out of line."

"You were saying about these magical attacks," said Emmeline. She stepped over to the bed and sat down next to Jeannie, putting an arm around the younger girl's shoulder and so, with unconscious witchcraft of the highest order, immediately turning her petulance into immense satisfaction. "What are they exactly?"

Alison frowned at the fair broad open face of her friend. Alison had always admired Emmeline's willingness to listen and learn—but where matters of dark arts

were concerned she did wish Emmeline would do these
things more in the style of an apprentice sorceress and
less like a student nurse.

She hunched her own head more than she might
otherwise have done, and rolled her eyes this way and
that, and lowered her voice to a near-croak.

"A magical attack is when another witch makes war
on you," she whispered.

"But *what* other witch, Alison?" asked Jeannie, nes-
tling closer to Emmeline with a thrilled shudder.

"*Any* other witch. Who knows? There are witches"—
Alison, still hunched, half turned to the window—"all
over, everywhere, even in the city, *especially*"—she was
staring hard at a certain window, still in darkness—"in
the city."

Emmeline nodded placidly.

"Yes, sure. Like in *Rosemary's Baby*."

"Did *you* get to see *that?*" gasped Jeannie. "What was
it like, Emmeline? You can tell me *now*. Now I'm a
witch myself."

"Jeannie . . ."

"Sorry, Alison."

"This," hissed Alison, dropping her voice even lower,
"could be worse, more dangerous, more—horrible—than
any old *Rosemary's Baby*."

Some of the placidity left Emmeline's face. She shiv-
ered slightly.

"Oh, come *on*," she said. "It couldn't be, Alison. It—"

"And I say it could. The way it's been shaping up.
I mean—listen . . ."

Then, ticking each item off on her fingers, she went

through them again: the signs, the symptoms, the por-
tents, the things that had gone wrong in so many ways,
ever since their return to New York.

"I mean, not only to me, by body, my—my *person*,"
she prefaced this sinister inventory, "but to my belongings they've gone wrong. And not only to my ordinary
belongings but also to my witch equipment. And sometimes there's been a chain of things, one starting off another. And there've been things going wrong to things
around me—to growing things as well as mechanical
things—and to—oh, I guess you'd call it general circumstances. To them, too, things have gone wrong. . . ."

And there was no denying she had a point, several
points, some twenty points in all.

For, of mishaps to her person, there had been:

> the losing of a filling from a side tooth, while
> eating *custard*, of all things;
>
> the breaking of a fingernail while unpacking her
> suitcase;
>
> the biting of her tongue while protecting the
> cavity while eating a far too gristly hamburger;
>
> a toe stubbed so badly that the nail had gone
> black.

Then, moving on in the wake of the attacks, the
following disasters had befallen her ordinary belongings:

> she had torn a hole in her very best, nearly
> new, red quilted-calico shorts with the broad
> suspenders, the right one of which had caught

in a nail at the side of this very window, a nail which she could have sworn had never been there before, painted the same color as the woodwork though it was; and

she had lost her second-best purse on the way back from school, containing 78 cents and a lucky subway token.

Yet even these had been mere mild annoyances compared to the accidents ("Accidents? Huh! *Some* accidents!") to her witch belongings:

the splitting of one of the bulbs of her Necklace, for absolutely no natural reason, leaving only twelve unless she bought another in New York (which she hadn't dared to do in case its alien vibrations destroyed the magic of the surviving originals);

the equally inexplicable chipping, en route from West Salem, of the Magic Mirror, heavily swathed in dirty towels though it had been;

the spilling of black ink ("as if an invisible hand or *claw* had clutched my elbow") over her Workbook ("though this just *might* have been a separate happening, a friendly reminder from Ariadne M. that I should have stuck to green");

the final snapping of the rubber bands of her Garter (though they had been going one by one for some time); and then (here was where

the chain reaction came in), when she'd found
a red velvet hair band that would do much
better,

the discovery by her mother of the handbell,
and being made to mail it back to the house in
West Salem; followed by:

the strange inability to track down a substitute
bell in the whole of their New York apartment
or any of the cheap stores nearby.

The growing thing (there was actually only the one)
to go wrong had been her rubber plant, given to her
nearly a year ago by their most handsome uncle—Ray—
who'd promised her a dollar for every extra leaf it put
out in her care. Having survived the casual attention
of the cleaning lady for the whole of the summer, it
had suddenly started wilting, then drooping, within
two days of Alison's return, and had still shown no
signs of recovery.

As for the mechanical troubles, these included:

the constant slowing down of her watch;

the repeated fuse-blowing and final breakdown
of the air conditioner in her room, during this,
one of the hottest Septembers on record; and

being stuck in the building's elevator *two whole
hours* between floors 3 and 4, on her own, on
the way home from school. (But oh, oh, what a
transformation that would have been, what a
turning of the tables on her secret enemy, if

only Greg Peters, the boy from Apartment 4C,
voted unanimously by all her friends as the best-
looking senior at their school, had been trapped
with her there!)

Which brings us to the *circumstances* that had col-
lapsed about her ears:

for Greg Peters was not in that elevator at that
time, despite the fact that he could have been
and sometimes was, because he was just then
too busy walking home that mousy-haired thick-
ankled Nan Stafford from Seventy-third Street,
which in itself was a massive piece of bad luck in
Alison's reckoning; and

returning to school, looking forward to having
young Miss Deward as her homeroom teacher,
only to learn that she'd gone to live in a
commune in Maine, her homeroom duty being
taken over by that grotesque museum-piece Miss
Timmins.

"So there it is!" growled Alison bitterly. "All in the
space of two weeks. I mean, what else can it be? And
that's not to mention the dreams, the nightmares, the
—uh-huh!"

During her recital she had been continually glancing
out of the window. Now she froze, making the others
stiffen.

"What—what have you seen, Alison?" whispered Jeannie.

"There!" Alison continued to hold herself very still.

"Slowly, very, very slowly, come here and I'll show you."

When they had ranged themselves at her side, she said:

"Pretend to be looking across at those two dumb boys in the window over there, but slide your eyes to the right, to the old building, to the bay window with the yard—"

"Oh, yes!" whispered Emmeline. "I was meaning to ask you—"

"Where the old hermit woman's gone?" Alison shrugged. "I wouldn't know. She was there before we went on vacation. I remember thinking about her one day. But not since we've been back have we seen her. Or her cat. Right, Jeannie?"

"Right. There's only been this young one who's looking out now."

"Who's looking out most times if you ask me," muttered Alison. "In the morning, afternoons, late at night— you name it."

"I like her wig; I like that shade of blonde," said Emmeline enviously.

"How d'you know it's a wig?" asked Jeannie.

"Sometimes"—Alison was still muttering thoughtfully, not with her companions at all just then—"sometimes she looks as if she's making notes."

"I think she's pretty," said Jeannie.

"*Pretty!*" Alison almost spat the word, causing Norton, walking in and out of Emmeline's legs, to leap and spit in return, and Emmeline, in reaction to him, to squeak.

"There," said Alison, pointing to the cat, "*he* knows.

Norton knows there's something very far from pretty under *that* wig."

"Whu-what do you mean, Alison?" asked Jeannie.

"Yes?" said Emmeline, all still herself now.

"I mean that I can *feel* it, I can tell, I can feel it stronger than ever, right now, I *know* it. *I mean that she's the one!*"

As if to confirm Alison's statement—as if indeed some magical current had carried the girl's intense murmur across the thickening space, preserving it from obliteration by the sounds of traffic and aircraft, and amplifying it under the folds of that bright blonde hair—the woman's face turned and stayed fixed, looking directly up at them.

"She—she's seen us!" whispered Emmeline.

"Oh, Norton!" gasped Jeannie, swooping to the cat, whether to seek or give protection even she herself probably didn't know.

"Straighten yourself!" hissed Alison. "And look up there, at the boys—anywhere so she doesn't know we were watching *her.*"

They did this, all three heads—four if Norton, struggling in Jeannie's arms, was to be included—jerking convulsively around and away from the bay window below. But their eyes still flitted in that direction.

And what they saw was like a mocking reflection. With a toss of the bright hair, the woman's head had jerked away also—except that hers went in exactly the opposite direction, downwards and to their right. It was too far across for them to see clearly the eyes in that sallow oval blur of a face. The dusk was thickening almost visibly and the light behind her was dim, as if it came from a room behind the one she was standing in. But Alison didn't need to see those eyes to know that they too would be swiveled under her eyelashes and trained straight back at the window across.

She felt a tightening in her chest, and for a moment, as she tried to speak, she had the panicky fear that she'd been firmly entrapped in a tongue-binding spell.

Then she managed to gasp out:

"Now . . . quite . . . casually—make it casual—without looking at her . . . turn away from the window —ready?—and step back."

They did this. It was a ragged movement, with Emmeline treading on Jeannie's toes, and Jeannie yelling, and the cat squirming and clawing and making her yell again. But as they sat together, breathing heavily, on the edge of the bed away from the window, Alison felt that it had probably looked natural enough.

"And now," she said, after a few minutes, "I'm going to get up and pull down the blinds. Jeannie, go switch the light off first. Emmeline, you stay there till we're ready."

Only when the light had been switched off and the venetian blinds pulled down did the three girls go back to the center of the window again. Then Alison lifted a slat to make the thinnest of cracks and they peered directly down and across.

"This way she won't be able to see us," she explained.

But once again they had an eerie sensation of being mocked in reflection. For the shades had been lowered in the bay window too. Not venetians there, just ordinary cloth shades of a yellowish gray that would probably have looked dirty even in full daylight, one to each of the three sections.

"And who's to say *she* isn't watching through a crack?" whispered Alison, with a slight chattering of the teeth.

CHAPTER 15

The Fetch Sent Forth

Against a magical attack there were certain defenses, according to the author of *The Secret Arts of Witchcraft*. And now that Alison was sure not only that such an attack had been launched against her, but also that it had been directed by a certain recognizable person, she read the relevant chapter very carefully indeed. (For she had, of course, brought the book home with her, satisfying her conscience—and any unwritten law of witchcraft against stealing such an important object—by specially purchasing in the village store a copy of *Fifty Old Westchester Recipes* with which to replace it on the attic bookshelf.)

Among the most potent defenses recommended in the Witch Book were the following:

> the hanging of a holystone over the hearth;

> the suspending from the ceiling of a green glass ball used by sea fishermen to float their nets with;

> the nailing of a horsehoe over door or window, curved side under;

the placing of a pair of horns in a similar position;

the hanging of an iron key, the bigger and heavier the better, over one's bed;

the disposal of *any* iron objects around windows or doors—that metal being the active ingredient in such defense work; and

the setting of a Witch Bottle—a jar full of bent pins—under the bed.

Alison made a list of these articles directly after supper on the night that she and Emmeline and Jeannie had formed their conclusions about the Bay Window Woman (as they began to call her). Then, shortly before going to bed, she checked again.

The holystone, she decided with regret, was out. It might take her weeks to track one down in New York, and by then (here she treated herself to a delicious shiver down the back of her neck), it could be too late. And besides—where was the *hearth*?

She crossed the item off her list.

It was with even deeper regret that she rejected the Witching Ball. Somewhere at the back of her mind she remembered seeing green glass floats in various junk shops in the neighborhood, and the thought merely of possessing one gave her a warm thrill. But even this would entail a search, if she (remembering the difficulty over the Garter bell) knew anything about it. Things you *thought* you'd seen quite often usually turned out to be scarcer than you'd imagined. And again, time—even a matter of half a day or so—was vital, quite apart from the fact that some sixth witch sense was warning her: *Do not try anything that might be the least bit difficult while thou art under Attack. It giveth the Enemy more chances to trip thee up.*

She crossed that item off her list.

Horseshoes fared the same. Again she thought she'd seen them often enough in junk shops, but to be really sure she figured she would have to go over to the Police Stables in Central Park. And even then, if the Bay Window Woman knew her job, there might be a hex on the place, causing any policeman she approached to say: "Horseshoes? Think we've nothin' better to do than hand out horseshoes to any civilian comes askin'? Beat it, kid!" Yes, indeed. She could almost hear him saying it. And the laughing whinny his horse would give to speed her on her way. The Enemy would have taken care of horseshoes, all right.

She crossed that item off her list, congratulating herself on her wiliness in avoiding an obvious trap.

Horns?

"Schmorns!" she muttered, not even bothering to consider them further before crossing them off, so keen was she now to get down to practicalities. For hadn't the author of the Witch Book been speaking to her, deep to deep, with her remarks about *any* iron objects being effective? No doubt it had cost her—that fussy Timminslike teacherish person—to give her student witches so much leeway, making it so easy for them. But Ariadne Atropos Arachne could think of dozens of iron objects that could be purchased quite cheaply within a couple of blocks of the apartment. And after all, wasn't it time the city students had a break?

"I mean, *we* can't go out and dig up mandrake roots on Seventy-fifth Street," she said, addressing the old yellow-edged pages and fancying she could see in them the hair of the author, gray-white with tobacco-colored streaks. "And where would I find all these herbs for a special Sachet of Safety?"

But she did know where to find an empty honey jar and a quantity of pins, and that night, instead of counting sheep, she sat up in bed bending these pins with the aid of her nail scissors, and dropping them into the jar, and finding the tiny but clear *plink-plinking* every bit as sleep-inducing as the sheep watching. Twice she nearly nodded off with the task unfinished, but finally the last one was bent and deposited, to glitter sharply with the rest when lidded and shaken and pushed under the bed—at the side nearest the window, at the end nearest the Enemy.

She slept that night without a single dream, let alone another in the series of nightmares she'd been having; and in the morning, highly pleased with herself, she went out and made her purchases. As she'd realized, there was no shortage of iron in the neighborhood shops, but since it was Saturday and the combination of a good night's sleep and the bright morning sun had made her feel more secure, she took her time and chose thoughtfully.

The result was that she returned to the apartment at the end of ninety minutes with a length of heavy chain, a padlock as big as her hand, and—more precious than horns or horseshoe, Witching Ball or holystone—a hammerhead.

She placed the chain over her door with two nails, so that it hung glittering there like a Christmas festoon. She hung the padlock centrally above the window, again using two nails so that it could go upside down and thus, in a way, double as a horseshoe.

And she hung the hammerhead on the wall over the bed, using her wine-dyed Girdle Cord to suspend it by.

"The chain is pure protection," she explained to the wondering Jeannie and Emmeline, when she'd got it all fixed. "It says: 'Keep out or be hanged!' The padlock is part protection and part defiance. It says: 'Send what curse thou wilt to the Police Stables in Central Park, but beware lest the horseshoe shape will stamp upon thy forehead and brand thee as mine Enemy for all eternity!' "

(Alison had to look down at her Workbook to read this last statement, where, with the others, after being carefully composed, it had been recorded in green with a thousand flourishes and spirals. And as she looked down, Emmeline and Jeannie exchanged awed glances, wondering what the Police Stables had to do with it all.)

"But the hammerhead—that's the best, sisters. Because I never really expected to find him, didn't even know to look for him, yet there he was and when I saw him I knew he was for me. And you know what *he* says?"

Alison looked from the object itself to each of her companions with such fiery-browed ferocity that they flinched.

"He says: 'Dare to attack Ariadne Atropos Arachne while she sleeps and thou wilt be hammered to a bloody pulp!'"

"Wow!" gasped Jeannie.

"Yes," said Alison, "and he only cost a dollar twenty-five."

The rest of the day went without a single mishap, so it really did begin to look as if Ariadne Atropos Arachne's defenses were working well. In fact, not only did nothing go wrong for her or her two companions-in-craft, but the power of the iron seemed quite to have cowed the Enemy. Not once, in all the dozens of times the girls looked across, did the woman show her face that day. The yellow-gray shades remained down and perfectly motionless—so still that it was easy to believe that the woman wasn't risking even so much as a peep.

Emmeline and Jeannie were jubilant about this. They considered the battle to be over, the Enemy routed. But while she accepted their admiration and congratulations, Alison had a feeling that she had not heard the last of the Bay Window Woman. In her own mind she described this as an *uneasy* feeling: "Ariadne Atropos Arachne had an uneasy feeling that she had not heard the last of the Bay Window Woman." But it gave her such tremors of delight, this feeling, that she cherished it and nourished it until it grew into something different, bloated, bladderlike. It became an UNEASY feeling, with an UNEASY face to match. (One eyebrow down, the eye half closed, even as she laughingly accepted the others' congratulations, with a twitching upwards of the corner of the mouth beneath that eye.)

Perhaps it was unfair, then, to blame the pins in the bottle for not protecting her dreams a second night, whatever she might have thought of the failure of the hammerhead. For, by Alison's courting of her feeling, the pins were put in the same position as so many sentries—numerous, alert, with bayonets ready, sharpened and fixed—when the personage they're supposed to be guarding slips in or out of their ranks and issues challenges to the Enemy without consulting them.

At any rate, those challenges didn't go unheard. That Saturday night, after a day of surface victory, Alison had the worst nightmare of the recent series.

It had been pretty much the same each time: one of those faceless terrors of which no single concrete detail could ever be recalled, but with the horror and helplessness being more vivid than any she had experienced in more realistic dreams. Time and again she tried to reconstruct it in her mind, attempting to put it into words, like a story, and, when that failed, into pictures, as in a movie, which was more hopeless than ever. That night its strength was such that—though it still lacked any definite shapes or contours to fix her mind upon —she was at least able to trace a *sequence* when trying to describe it afterwards. And this was that sequence:

At first there was Nothing. Then, from somewhere beyond the edge of this Nothing, there came Something. This Something was not an article or a person or an animal. This Something was a happening. It was a happening that had already happened somewhere else. This Something that was going to happen again was a certain set of actions and reactions happening to quite simple, ordinary things maybe, but in a very special order or pattern. And it was this pattern of actions that was so monstrous, dreadful, terrifying—not the objects themselves. That much was certain. This Something was, in other words, rather like a tornado in its dreadfulness—just bits and pieces of very ordinary harmless things whipped up into one very dreadful thing. Alison couldn't tell what these ordinary things were in this case, because the Something that was to happen again, this time in her presence, hadn't happened before in her presence. Yet she knew for sure in the dream that very soon this Something that had happened before somewhere else, with the most terrible—oh, but the most terrible—results, was very soon going to happen in her presence, maybe actually *to* her, or at least involving her. But because she didn't know exactly—or even roughly—what that Something was, and because she didn't know exactly what kinds of things were going to be involved, there was no way of tracking it or evading it.

No way.

And then—at this stage of the dream, marked by this sudden crumpling sense of hopelessness—the Something began to advance (or descend, or ascend, or all three) from beyond the edge of Nothing. And so ferocious was this advance (or descent, or ascent, or movement in all three directions) that it tore the Nothingness to shreds, trailing it in ribbons behind it, so that the

Nothingness itself became part of the Something, and —and—AND—

At that point, heart thumping, mouth straining to take in air and give out screams, resulting in a silent working of the jaws, and with her hair all clammy with sweat, and the bed covers kicked off, Alison awoke.

It was the usual point at which she awoke.

As usual, she lay on her back, breathing heavily.

As usual, she tried, after blinking herself into consciousness, to work out a plan for defeating the creature or creatures of her dream so that she could go back and end it *her* way.

As usual, with this nightmare, she failed, the creature or creatures having no definite form—nothing to kick or grip or shoot at or turn a fatal creature-destructor ray on.

And then she heard it.

Not in her head this time.

Somewhere outside, beyond the silent air conditioner and through the open window.

Not—she froze—*not on the fire escape?*

But no . . .

There it came again. A faint, dull, scratching, scuffling noise, from farther below, with no hint of metal in it.

Slowly—fortified by the thought that the window had been specially fixed to allow no human form to get through its opening, and picking up her bottle of pins, more for actual physical protection as a missile than for any magical purpose—she went to the window.

There was a three-quarter moon. The buildings opposite

could be seen quite clearly. Instinctively she looked
toward the bay window. All seemed quiet there. The
shades were still down. There was no light from any
chink. In the little yard, the shadows around the iron
table were black, but without any movement whatsoever.

And yet the furtive sound continued—the slow scuffling, the scratching—and it came from somewhere in
that direction. A cat? Norton himself perhaps?

Taking a risk, Alison released the catch that restricted
the window's opening. Then, slowly, her head going
forward with the window, she leaned out, peering through
the rails of the fire escape and praying that she'd not
been mistaken, that the sounds weren't coming from
somewhere nearer than she'd figured—from the fire escape
itself.

And then she saw it.

No—thank heavens, thank Ariadne M., thank the shade
of Norton, thank all her magical protectors and pro-
tectresses!—not anywhere near her, but far below, down
there, slowly climbing the wall from the area on this
side to the yard of the bay window apartment on that
side—the small shadowy figure of a man.

Or was it a boy?

Or a midget?

Or—what?

It reached the top. It was dressed in black all over.
Dull black, nothing shiny. It stooped over the low fence
there, turned. Then it made strange bowing, swaying
movements that caused Alison to shiver and step back,
fearing she'd been seen and was being mocked.

When she looked again she was just in time to see

the last of the prowler slide over the low sill of the
middle window of the bay: a black leg and foot, or
arm and hand,—it was difficult to tell. But the window
must have been open after all, she decided, watching
the pale blind drop sideways and down, back into position.

She stared for several minutes, trying to fix in her
mind that last glimpse she'd had of the climber. *Had*
it been his leg? Or was it an unusually long arm? Again
through her mind went the alternatives: man, boy,
midget, beast. . . .

Had it been a—a *tentacle* of some kind?

Then all at once she remembered her dream, and her
adversary in witchcraft, and this in turn reminded her
of something she'd read recently in the book—something
she hadn't paid too much attention to at the time.

Refixing the safety catch of the window, she went
over to her desk and got the book and the red flashlight.
Then, returning to her bed, she made a tent of the
covers and switched on the light.

The book came open at the very page she was seeking.
She bent closer and read the passage she'd half remembered. As she did so, her heart began to beat faster
and the sweat started from her forehead again.

For this was what the passage said:

*Beware of joining battle with the most advanced
witches, however, for they are skilled in Sending Forth
the Fetch. So great are the powers of such practition-
ers that they can project them into a definite shape—
sometimes animal, sometimes human, sometimes an*

amalgam, always dangerous. Such shapes are called Fetches, and they can be sent forth by the witches creating them, to wreak havoc on their enemies— especially at night. . . .

CHAPTER 16

Counterattack

"A *what?*" asked Emmeline, giving a little scream.

"A *Fetch*," said Alison. "And keep your voice down. We're supposed to be doing our homework together, remember."

"It's a kind of—a—a whoojum—a ghost-type thing—a—"

"Jeannie, be quiet. You don't know what you're talking about."

"Well, *you* told me about them. I'm only saying what—"

"And you're interrupting again. And you're supposed to be in your own room, cleaning up the mess that Norton made and got into trouble for, all because you were dumb enough to shut him in all day away from his litter."

"I've cleaned it already."

"I bet you have."

Alison gave Jeannie a last glance of deep disgust before turning back to Emmeline. The McNair family had been away visiting friends in Port Washington most of that Sunday, while Emmeline and her family had been making their weekly trip to see an old uncle in Rye, and this was the first chance Alison had had of telling her friend about the mysterious prowler of the previous night.

"A Fetch is far more dangerous than any old ghost," she said. "Listen . . ."

Emmeline listened as Alison read out from the book the passage on Fetches. The fair-haired girl's blue eyes widened with every syllable—widened and slowly turned to the window where, once again, dusk was falling, deepening the violet strip between the new building and the old.

"Gosh!" she whispered when Alison had finished. "And you think that's what this"—she shuddered—"this dark thing was?"

"I'm sure of it," said Alison, nodding gravely, enjoying Emmeline's reaction but not forgetting her own horror of the night before. "It was a Fetch. Sent by *her*."

The three girls gazed out and down at the bay window. It was still unlit, still masked by the dirty shades.

Jeannie's eyes went into slits, the way she used to peer into the Magic Mirror.

"Maybe she's a Fetch herself," she said, in a slow trancelike voice that caused Alison to catch her breath and look at her sister closely. "Maybe she's the old woman's Fetch—the old hermit woman we haven't seen since we went away. Maybe the old woman's sick in bed with her cat lying on her chest like a round heavy stone with moss on it, and—"

"Oh, but—" Emmeline began, but Alison, still looking at Jeannie, put out a hand to check her friend.

"Go on," murmured Alison.

"Maybe the old woman can't move out of her bed and

she sends this Fetch in the shape of the young woman
with the wig to the window, and then the young woman
Fetch sends this other Fetch—"

"No, no, *no!*" insisted Emmeline.

She was shaking her head firmly.

Alison, who was becoming intrigued by this Double
Fetch theory of her sister's, looked at Emmeline with
slight annoyance.

"Why not?" demanded Jeannie, indignantly echoing
Alison's own objection.

"Because I know all about her," said Emmeline, looking very complacent and round and newly washed. "Because this morning I made a few inquiries."

"Huh!" grunted Alison. "This is a witch matter, not a
detective thing."

Emmeline had had a leaning toward private eye adventures for a long time now, and being very unlike
Alison, she had an irritating (to Alison) way of persisting
in her leanings.

"Oh, well, if you don't want to hear what I've found
out about her—"

"Oh, yes, *please*, Emmeline. What?" asked Jeannie.

Once again the younger girl had echoed her sister's
own feelings. Nevertheless, Alison kept her face calm and
aloof and quite uninterested—knowing full well that Emmeline wouldn't be able to keep her findings to herself
anyway.

"Well," said Emmeline, pointedly addressing Jeannie
only, "I was getting some baclava to take to Uncle
Bob—it's his favorite and we always take him some every
Sunday—"

"Oh, get on!" snapped Alison.

"Well," continued Emmeline, absolutely unruffled and still addressing Jeannie, "I met Vivienne Hertz in the deli, and I remembered she lives in that same building, only in the front, higher up—"

"Does she?" said Jeannie. "I didn't—"

"Don't interrupt!" said Alison. She was looking very interested now as she turned to her friend. "Go on, Emmeline. I'm sorry about that."

"That's O.K., Ally." Emmeline looked positively radiant now as she began addressing Alison at last. "Well, I asked Viv first about the old woman with the cat, and she told me she'd left ages ago, on the twenty-third of July, to go live with her daughter in New Jersey somewhere, and the Bay Window Woman took over five days later."

"How did—"

"—she know so exactly?" cut in Emmeline, in a way that usually made Alison go wild with irritation. Not now though. "That's what I asked her. And she said the dates and things were carved forever on the hearts of all the family—you know how she talks—because they were hoping to rent that place themselves for Viv's own grandmother, and they thought they had it all lined up. You see, the super had promised it to them, and then he went back on his promise and let this woman have it instead."

"She'd put a spell on him!" said Alison, darkly.

"You bet!" said Jeannie.

Emmeline smiled her placid· open smile and shook her head.

"Oh, no . . . No. No spell. Not *your* sort, anyway. No.

Viv told me what happened. She said this woman must be very rich. She said they knew she must because Mr. Hertz had promised the super a hundred dollars—and when they heard about the woman coming they said they'd double it. And the super just laughed, and he kept on laughing even when they'd pushed it up to three hundred, and he said they were batting in the wrong league."

"Hm," murmured Alison. "Well . . . with *that* one mixed up in it, it could still be a spell. I mean a witch as powerful as that could give the man ten one-dollar bills and charm him into thinking they're hundreds. . . . Anyway, that's all history, past, done with. She's there—attacking me, us, with everything she's got—and what we have to think about is the future."

Emmeline looked around at the chain and the hammerhead and the inverted padlock.

"Maybe we—you don't need anything else, Alison. Maybe you've done enough."

"After last night's experience? You can say *that?* Huh! I wish she'd start interfering with *your* dreams. I wish she'd send the Fetch up *your* fire escape."

"In—in the daytime they work, though—don't they?" ventured Jeannie.

"Yesterday they did. Sure. But aren't you forgetting what happened today? About Norton?"

"Oh, that! But that was my fault, really."

"Your fault or not, I got part of the bawling out, didn't I? . . . I tell you that one is one of the *top* witches. And I'll tell you something else. I wouldn't mind betting she's got something of mine. To make her attacks this powerful. With a Fetch and all."

"Got something?" asked Emmeline.

"Yes. A snipping of hair, or some of my nail clippings, or—I don't know—anything. Maybe a photograph. That's how they operate."

"Like with bloodhounds," said Jeannie, suddenly grave, nodding.

"Eh?"

Even Alison had been pulled up by that."

"Like with bloodhounds. She'll give that Fetch something of yours to sniff so it knows where to—"

"No, *no*," said Alison. "That wouldn't be necessary. But if she's got something of mine on her Altar while she's casting her spells or making her curses, it'll make it so much more powerful."

"Well—"

Emmeline hesitated, her eyes flitting nervously to the window.

"Well what?"

"Oh, nothing . . . no. It would probably not work if *you* did it."

"What wouldn't?" said Alison, bridling. "Go on. Say it now you've started it."

"I was just thinking . . . why don't you get something of hers and curse her back?"

Alison was taken by surprise, but she quickly covered all traces of it.

"Oh," she said, shrugging. "Well . . . yes . . . I've been thinking along those lines myself."

"*Have* you, Alison?" Jeannie asked eagerly. "That's a *great* idea!"

Emmeline picked up confidence.

"We could ask Vivienne to get something from the woman's trash can," she said. "Why don't we?"

Alison's lip curled.

"Certainly *not!*" she said. "This is strictly between us and that woman. In fact *really* strictly, it's between *me* and that woman. *I'll* do the getting."

"I'll help you," said Jeannie.

"You'll—" began Alison, turning on her sister with a fiercely scornful look. Then she changed her mind. "All right. You can help. By doing exactly as you're told. No more. No less."

"Yes. Sure. What do you want me to do?"

"I don't know yet. . . ."

Alison was gazing thoughtfully down at the bay window apartment. It was still light enough to pick out most of the details of the little square yard in front of it, raised up from the basement area on its own brick pedestal. This was the wall the Fetch had scaled the night before— about twenty feet high, she calculated, using her favorite measuring device of imagining policemen standing on each other's shoulders. Yes: from three to four cops high, she told herself. Which meant, taking into account the fairly even surface of the brickwork, that the Fetch must have been some climber. No wonder the image of tentacles had crossed her mind! Tentacles with powerful suckers at the end, that Fetch must have been equipped with. Unless—

Her eyes narrowed, as all at once she remembered the bowing movements—the swaying and bowing over the fence.

Unfastening something?

A *rope ladder?*

"What are you thinking about, Ally?" asked Emmeline tentatively.

"A plan," she growled. "For getting across there."

"Oh, I have a good idea for that," said Emmeline, all bright and sure of herself again. "Why don't we call Viv now and ask if we can stop by a minute to discuss this algebra thing we're supposed to be wrestling with? Then we could have a look outside the door of—"

"No!" said Alison. "I told you. This is *my* task."

"But you could be the one to—"

"I said *no!* How many more times? . . . Besides, she might not have left any trash outside her door yet, and then where would we be? . . . Oh, no!" Alison shook her head so vigorously that the flying wings of red hair brushed the faces of her companions, causing them to back away. "I have to be *absolutely* sure. And I know exactly how I can be. Look. See the iron table—where the old lady used to clean her spoons?"

They peered down through the dusk and nodded.

"There's something white on it," said Jeannie.

"Exactly," said Alison. "In fact, if it was a bit lighter you'd have seen there were *two* somethings white on it.

"Oh, yes!" said Emmeline. "I could have told you that. I noticed them when I first came over tonight. A pair of shoes."

"*Women's* shoes," Alison said portentously. "That's the important detail. *Hers*. She must have cleaned them and put them out to dry sometime earlier."

"Well, so what?" said Emmeline. "There's nothing sinister about—" Then her eyes widened. "Alison!" she gasped. "You're not thinking of—"

"I am," said Alison. She was enjoying the shock she'd produced. It made her all the more determined to proceed. "I mean, what better article could I have for *my* spells than one of her shoes?"

"But—that would be stealing!" said Jeannie.

"Borrowing," said Alison. "She can have it back when I've got the hex good and fast upon her. . . . If she *needs* shoes by then!"

"Alison," said Emmeline, in her most irritating, placidly cocksure manner, "there's just one thing against it."

"What?"

"How are you going to get into that yard? The only way is through the apartment window."

"Oh, yes? Well, how about up the wall?"

Emmeline smirked.

"Come *on*, Ally. You're no Fetch with legs like a fly."

"He," said Alison, "or It, used a ladder. A rope ladder. I've been figuring it out."

"Hmm!" Emmeline frowned. "You didn't tell us that. . . . But anyway, even if he did, it's not there now. And you still need to get into the yard to tie it into place, so—"

"So why don't you just be quiet for a minute and let me explain? I mean, who said anything about me using a *rope* ladder, huh? Listen, down in the basement there's an aluminum ladder."

"Oh, yes!" said Jeannie. "The one Mr. Hernandez used to—"

"—to climb that very wall," said Alison, her eyes gleaming as she looked at Emmeline. "When Norton—the first Norton—Norton in his first incarnation—when he got himself stranded up there one time, and the old lady wasn't home."

"But—you mean *you—now?*"

"Who else, when else?" said Alison. Already she was over at her dressing table, opening drawers and tumbling clothes about in search of a black cashmere sweater that, together with her dark blue jeans, would give her better camouflage than the bright yellow shirt she was wearing already. "It's Sunday, isn't it? No Hernandez. No one working in the area. . . . Ah, here it is."

"But supposing someone catches you? What will you say?"

"Oh, the usual. A lost ball . . ."

"At this time?"

"Er—we-e-ell . . ." For once Alison faltered, having to recognize grudgingly that Emmeline had a point. "We-e-ell . . ." Her eyes flitted about desperately as she pulled on her black sweater.

"*I* know!" cried Jeannie. "Norton! *This* Norton!"

"What?"

"Why not? Same as before. But this time you can take him up yourself. In that airline bag we brought him here in. He just loves being given a ride in that."

"Jeannie," said Alison, "no—Jezebel—that's one marvelous idea! I hereby declare you're a fully qualified Witch, from this moment on."

"Can I come with you then?"

"No. That's my task and 'tis mine alone. But thou canst be getting the animal ready."

Twenty minutes later, with the ladder propped securely against the wall and Emmeline holding it as an extra safeguard, Ariadne Atropos Arachne began her assault on the lair of her Enemy. In the black sweater and dark jeans, she merged fairly well with the shadows of the wall she was scaling, while Norton, crouched in the airline bag slung across her back by means of the wine-dyed Girdle Cord, seemed to be tolerating his ride if not exactly enjoying it.

The climb was steeper and shakier than Alison had imagined, but she took comfort from a number of things, like the support of Emmeline, whose face quickly became a pale round blur; and the fact that the area was so narrow at that point that even if the ladder did slip (oh, gosh! oh, *well!*) it would soon be brought to a stop by the opposite wall; and the warm hard feel of the bulbs around her neck under the sweater; and the bulkier touch and faint military rattle of the bottle of bent pins in her back pocket.

And when she reached the top and had got a leg safely over the low fence, she felt so elated that she took time off to blow a kiss to Emmeline below, and give an elaborate witchly wave—fist high, two fingers horned, twirled jerkily thrice—to Jezebel, who, as arranged, was watching it all through a slit in the blinds, somewhere above.

"Kraa!" came a bleat from behind Alison, just at that moment, nearly causing her to miss her footing.

Then she grinned and, gently patting the now rather vigorously lurching bag on her back, whispered:

"O.K., Norton, O.K. We'll soon be back home again."

But the sound of her voice seemed only to make the cat more fearful.

"Kraaa-ee-ow!" he bleated, this time so loud that she had to stop on her way to the table and ease the bag to the front, to make sure he wasn't halfway out.

He wasn't; the zipper was still closed to within an inch; yet it obviously made no difference.

"Yeeow! Yee*eeow!*" screeched the cat, and it was as if the canvas cover were acting as an amplifier. "Yee-ee-ee-eeow!"

"Please, Norton, *please!*" hissed Alison. "Just another half-minute and—"

She broke off in horror, suddenly dry at the throat, as the yard, the table, the white shoes, the chair, the litter of old plant pots and other junk became lit up and a window was opened and a woman's voice said:

"What are *you* doing out here?"

Alison turned, clutching her thumping wailing bundle, and blinked.

It was the woman with the wig, the Enemy, already with one leg across the low sill. And behind her another person, a man, was peering with malevolent surprise from the back of the room.

CHAPTER 17

In the Lair of the Enemy

"Well, don't just stand there. I asked you a question. What are you doing in here?"

The woman was in the yard now, standing with hands on hips, facing Alison, staring down at her. She was tall, thin, bony. She was wearing a green dress with black paisley patterns that curled and writhed like smoke in the dim light out there, putting Alison in mind of a witch beginning to burn at a stake. The woman's face had that sort of look, too: tense above the prominent neck sinews, taut around the grimacing mouth, and with a sickly yellowish-green cast of complexion that contrasted strongly with the yellow hair. As for the eyes, under the heavy green-painted lids—

But Alison looked quickly away from those eyes, knowing only too well from her researches in *The Secret Arts of Witchcraft* the dangers of a direct eye-to-eye confrontation with someone as adept in those arts as this woman obviously was.

"Well?"

"I—er—the cat," Alison mumbled, keeping her eyes on the woman's smoking dress in the region of the waistline and the long-fingered, silver-nailed, big-knuckled hands fixed there. "He—the tree over there—he must have climbed it—jumped off the limb. Looking for the cat that used to live here, I guess."

As her explanation took shape, gathering momentum, Alison began to feel easier. After all, she had come well prepared for this. In fact—she told herself, as she held out the bag and unzippered it enough for Norton to stick his head out—it would have been a waste and a pity if she hadn't had cause to use such a good excuse.

"Oh. I see."

The woman's voice softened a little as she stooped to the round gray head with the up-pricked ears. Alison caught a whiff of the woman's perfume—tangy, almost acrid—and so must Norton have, for his nose came up, sniffing curiously and, judging from his silence, even appreciatively. But that may have been because of his part release from the bag, Alison decided, with a slight twinge of jealousy, as the woman extended a silver nail and scratched the animal gently between the ears, murmuring:

"A little kitty, a purty little kitty."

Alison slowly drew back the bag, not wanting Norton to be won over to the other side completely.

The woman's expression was much less severe now as she straightened up and looked at Alison. There was almost something of relief in it. Then, even as the girl was thinking this and beginning to feel quite relaxed, the woman frowned, glancing up at the top of the ginkgo tree and the slender branch that curved over her yard.

"But how did *you* get here?"

"Yeah!" This last remark came from the window.

The woman turned, giving Alison a better view of the
man framed there. He was so small he might have been
mistaken for a boy at first glance, if it hadn't been
for the growly, husky deepness of his voice. He was
wearing a pale-gray and black striped bathrobe, and
there were streaks of white lather—shaving soap—on his
jaws under each ear. His eyes were oval and hard and
unblinking, and his hair was like a black close-fitting
cap, furry, catlike itself. "That's just what I been wondering," he said, stepping out into the yard. "How *did*
you get in here, kid?"

Alison shuddered, and Norton gave a low growl, ears
flattening, as the man approached. His legs and feet
were bare, making his progress a silent padding and his
whole gray and black person more catlike than ever.

"I—I used a ladder," Alison managed to gasp as she
backed off a little. "Fu-from the yard. My friend is
down there."

She added this last remark in the hope that it would
deter the cat-man from any drastic pouncing action he
might have been contemplating.

"Huh!"

He swerved and padded past her to the wall, bending
there and swaying as he peered into the shadows below.

That settled it for Alison.

Those movements, that silence—this was none other
than the Fetch of the previous night!

"There's a ladder all right," murmured the man, turning and addressing her softly. "But I don't see nobody
down there."

Alison didn't know whether to feel glad or perturbed

at that news. Obviously, Emmeline had heard the voices and retreated, scared, around a corner or into a recess somewhere. Maybe if she'd stayed put her presence would have deterred the man and woman from trying anything funny. But then again, maybe they were satisfied anyway and would now let her go.

The woman, at least, seemed satisfied.

"Well, you'd better not risk your neck twice, dear," she said. "Especially now you have a cat in your bag. Why don't you come through the apartment and out that way?"

Alison hesitated a moment. Was this a trap? The woman *seemed* genuine enough, but—

The man had other ideas.

"Aw, let her get down the way she came. Why should we worry?"

He produced a cigarette and lighter from his robe and padded back to the window, unconcerned.

"And maybe fall off this time?" The woman's voice was hard. "Use your head!"

He turned quickly, his eyes flashing up at the woman. Then he blinked and lowered his head and lit his cigarette.

"Yeah, sure, see what you mean. . . . O.K., honey." He blew smoke in a neat plume in Alison's direction. "Come on. Be our guest. Use this way out."

With a single, silent, agile bound, he re-entered the apartment.

Again Alison hesitated.

"After you, dear," said the woman, laying a hand on the girl's shoulder.

It was the lightest of touches, but electrifying.

Alison gave a slight jump, then stepped over the sill and into the apartment.

"Through here, through here."

She sighed with relief to hear the man's voice coming through the lighted doorway of the next room. At least he hadn't been waiting to pounce on her in there, in the darkened bedroom with its strange perfumes and dim looming shapes. She went on quickly, conscious of the other presence—probably the more dangerous one at that—just behind her; and then she was even more relieved to notice the very ordinary, rather untidy homeliness of the living room, with its sofa and chairs, its television set and bookcase and table and rubber plant and litter of Sunday newspaper supplements.

The man was standing by the main doorway, hand on the catch, so anxious was he to speed her on her way.

Alison felt she could take a little time off to be polite, to be cool, to have at least *that* much to boast about when telling the others of her encounter.

"Well, thank you very much, ma'am," she said, turning to the woman (though still being careful to avoid a direct eye-to-eye look). "It was kind of you to ask me through."

"Oh, forget it, dear." said the woman, stooping again to scratch Norton's head. "My pleasure. I had a cat of my own, once—kitty, kitty, kitty!" Norton purred, loud and deep and treacherously. The woman straightened up. "You say he used to come visiting with the old lady's cat?"

Completely lulled now, troubled only by Norton's

disgusting show of pleasure, Alison nodded. She was feeling much bolder, and it had occurred to her that she might even accomplish what she'd come over for, if she kept cool and played for time.

"Yes," she said brightly, concentrating more on the act of talking than on what she was saying. "Once he did. Last year our janitor had to get a ladder and rescue him when the old lady was out. That's what gave me the —the idea. . . ."

Alison faltered, wondering why the woman was frowning again, tense again, hipbones, knuckles, neck sinews all tight and jutting.

"Last year? But this is only just out of kittenhood. I tell you I know something about cats, and this is no more than six months old. Huh? So what's all this about rescuing him last year?"

There was a click behind Alison as the man closed the door again.

"Yeah?" he said, and his voice was a menacing purr that cut short Norton's happier rumblings at once. "You sure you tellin' us the truth, kid?"

"I—" Alison looked from one to the other, fighting to keep the smile on her lips, her eyes wide and her brow smooth. "Yes—well—you see—he died. He got killed by a taxi on Madison and—and then he came back from the dead."

"He—*what?*"

Whatever explanation the man had been expecting, that obviously had not been it. He gaped. Still gaping, he turned to the woman. She was smiling in a wrinkled-up way, equally surprised, but infinitely cooler.

"He came back from the *dead?*"

"Yes." Alison's lips tightened. Encouraged by the confusion she'd caused, she'd decided to give the Enemy due warning of her *own* considerable powers. "I *charmed* him back to life. I organized a Dumb Supper. I have very special powers. And one of these nights," she added, encouraged further by their expressions, "I am going to Send Forth a Fetch myself."

And enter that *in your Magical Workbook!* she thought, staring about her defiantly.

"Send forth a *what?*" whispered the man.

Alison ignored him. Looking at the woman straight between the neck sinews, she said:

"*You* know, don't you? A Fetch. A creature who will creep out at night and do mine bidding. Fetch me whatever I ask," she concluded, with the slightest of knowing sneers for the man.

"Hey!" gasped the man, flashing his eyes up at the woman. "You think she—?"

Some gesture of the woman's made him go quiet and dip his head and reach for an ashtray to stub his cigarette in.

Alison turned—supremely confident now—and, smiling sweetly, said to the woman:

"I would like to go to the bathroom. May I use yours?"

The man nearly choked over his last mouthful of smoke.

"The huck-huh-hell ya can!"

The woman frowned at him. With an effort, she smiled at Alison.

"Yes, sure, dear. Go ahead."

"But—" The man bounded forward, bringing himself between the girl and the door the woman had indicated.

Again the woman gestured.

"She's just a *child*, Harry. Leave her be."

Just a child indeed! thought Ariadne Atropos Arachne as, head high, smirking, she went into the bathroom, taking the cat with her, lest he be got at, lest that in fact had been the reason for the Enemy's willingness to allow her in there. *Aha!* and *Oho!* she thought. *But in Ariadne Atropos Arachne the Enemy had an adversary too cunning by far to be caught out like that!*

She locked the door carefully and looked around. She hadn't really wanted to go to the toilet, of course. She had other work to do. . . .

The bathroom was in a mess. There were women's tights drying over the edge of the tub, and dirty towels on the floor. The washbowl was half full of scummy water, and there was a soapy safety razor on the ledge between the faucets. On a shelf above that was a row of jars and bottles: hand creams, face creams, perfumes, deodorants.

Alison shook her head, feeling she might do better than that. She looked under the washbowl and gave a hiss of pleasure at seeing the wastebasket, crammed with dirty tissues, old jars, and heaven knew what else. She lifted it out, quickly scrabbled through it, and then:

"Just the very thing!" she whispered to the craning head of Norton, who was still in the bag, which she'd placed by the door.

She was holding a ball of hair and fluff, the scrapings from a brush. The hair was a mousy brown, coarse, and long, not short and black and soft like the man's.

"It has to be *hers!*" she whispered, carefully squeezing it and putting it in the pocket not already occupied by the bottle of bent pins.

Then she felt like washing her hands, which she did under a running faucet after gingerly releasing the plug from the depths of the scummy water. What she didn't feel like, however—she decided, looking around with a wrinkled nose—was drying her hands on any of *those* towels.

And that was how she came to look in the closet by the door—not because she was snooping, for she'd already got what she wanted, but simply to find a clean towel.

Sure enough, clean towels there were, in neat stacks on slatted shelves. Quickly—eager now to be home to tell her tale of triumph and display her trophy—she flicked at the edges, instinctively in search of the smallest hand towels.

"No need to make too much extra laundry, even for *her*," she murmured. "And—"

She stopped, her hand on a pink towel which she'd pulled part way from the pile, and stared.

Shivers, prickles—she couldn't tell what—started up at the back of her neck then, without any coaxing from her. For, with the pink towel, out had come another piece of colored material—but stiff, not soft, and blazing and flickering and glowing and shining with many colors, rich colors, living colors, not just one simple everyday dye.

Too startled to touch it, she could do no more than stare at the one long corner she had exposed—at the small grave faces of men in robes, and the flash of spurs and the tips of scabbards, and some boots with pointed upcurling toes. And (this is what had particularly sent shivers to her back) although it was not the actual scene she had at last made out in the Magic Mirror that day in West Salem, it was very similar to it, so similar that she felt it must be the final working of a spell—a witchly trap that had been laid long ago and was now to spring about her and imprison her forever, probably in that very scene itself, making her just another face in the crowd behind the grave courtiers and soldiers.

"Hey! What're you *doing* in there?"

Oddly enough, the man's voice came as a glimmer of comfort. At least she could still jump, she told herself. The shrinking and fixing had obviously not started to operate. Surprised to find her hands had quite dried without the help of a towel, she shut the closet door at once.

"I'm sorry," she said, going out into the living room. Her voice was shaking a little, she noticed. She took a firmer grip on the cat bag. "I'm sorry if I've kept you waiting." They were watching her, neither of them speaking. "Thank you—for letting me use the bathroom. Thanks. I'll—I'd better be going now."

This time it was the woman who was standing by the door, her hand on the catch.

"Yes, well . . ." she said, frowning thoughtfully.

"Oh, no, you don't!"

The man's voice sounded hollow as it came through the doorway of the bathroom.

"Keep that door shut," he said, coming back. He glared at Alison. "You've been snoopin' around, haven't you, kid?"

Behind her, the woman gasped.

"She—she hasn't been into—?"

"Yeah! That's just what she *has*. I warned you not to let her in."

"But—"

"The towels. *I* know how I leave things. I'm no slob like—argh! anyway—there's a corner of the picture showing. Go see for yourself."

In three soft, barefooted strides he was over by the main door himself. He gave the woman an impatient push as she moved toward the bathroom, shaking her head.

Alison clutched the cat bag tighter than ever in one hand and put her other hand around the pin bottle in her hip pocket, for whatever comfort and support it might be able to provide. She was still dazed, still puzzled. But now her terror was returning. Even Norton had started to wail again.

The woman reappeared at the door of the bathroom. She looked very thoughtful. She was rubbing a wrist, as if there were a bracelet on it that was chafing her.

"This changes things," she murmured. "We'd best leave right away."

"You bet we had!" the man snarled softly. "But

what about *her?* We can't let her go blabbering it around."

The woman nodded. The heavy eyelids came down like small silvery-green shutters. Alison quickly looked away.

"We'll just have to see she stays quiet for an hour or so. That should give us a good enough start." The voice hardened, became crisp. "Hold her while I find something to tie her with. Towels should do."

Alison had been thinking. Whatever it was, the picture she'd seen was the cause of her predicament. And thinking of it in those terms—simply as "a picture"—had made her remember something else: the memory behind the memory. That scene in the Magic Mirror. That too had been a picture! Of course! It had been one she'd seen on a school visit—a trip that had been made to the small private museum at the end of her own street: the Weinstock Collection. She hadn't paid too much attention to the pictures because of the very fact of the museum's being so near home. She'd been much more concerned with slipping out and getting home early, to lie in wait in the lobby and stage an "accidental" meeting with Greg Peters, merely for the pleasure of riding up in the elevator with him.

The Weinstock Collection. The same block. The same back areas. The Fetch's journey . . .

The connection flashed through her mind in the time it took for the woman to turn back to the bathroom and for Alison to unscrew the lid of the pin bottle.

Then, even as she backed away and the man started forward, she was spilling those bent pins on the rug between them.

"Hey! What—"

The man broke off with a howl as his bare foot padded full down in the thick of the pins. Alison threw the empty jar at his head and yelled herself—for help—as she headed for the bedroom door. Norton's wail rose to a wild scream, and again the man howled, as his other foot landed more heavily on the pins than the first, because it was hopping and so bearing more weight.

Alison slammed the door shut behind her, grateful that it had a modern handle, with only a button to press to lock it. Then she ran to the window, flung it open wide, snatched the shade aside, and jumped into the yard, still yelling for help and hoping that the man wouldn't burst open the door before she was safely down the—

Ladder!

Where?

"Oh, no!" she groaned, peering down.

But it was so.

The ladder was gone. There was no glimmer of it anywhere. Emmeline must have removed it, thinking to cover up in some way. But if she had—

Alison stared up at her own building, at the fire escape, trying to figure out which was her room.

"Emmie!" she screamed. "Help! Help! Emmie! Jeannie! Call the police! They're going to tie me up! They're thieves! They're going to drown me in the tub!"

This last bit was pure invention, of course, but since it was her own and she was Alison McNair, she believed it implicitly, and she screamed all the louder. "Help! *Help!* HELP!"

Lights were on everywhere. Windows were being flung open.

The battering at the door behind her took on a splintering noise.

"HELP!" she screamed. "Oh, HELP me! Please!"

A dark shape came leaping through the window. She crouched low against the fence, trembling.

"That's O.K., honey! Quiet down! You're safe now."

She opened her eyes and peered up at the dark arm. Light gleamed on the silvery stripes there.

"Su-sergeant?" she whispered.

"Maloney himself," murmured the policeman gently. "Come on now. Up you get. It's all over now."

Then she was led back into the apartment living room, still clutching Norton's bag, but with the cat now transferred, by some magic she'd not been aware of, into the brawny brown arms of another policeman. Then she recognized Vivienne Hertz, white-faced and round-eyed, and Mr. Hertz, and a man who might have been the super, judging from the way he was frowning at the damaged door. And then she saw another group by the bathroom door, half in, half out: the Bay Window Woman, her wig all to one side, and the Fetch man, and two more cops.

One of the latter was holding out the unframed picture.

"No need to ask what was causing all *this* hassle, Sarge. Lookit. A cool quarter-million bucks of oil painting, according to the description."

The sergeant shrugged.

"Personally, where it's pictures, I like the *Playboy* fold-outs best." He patted Alison's shoulder. "Come on, honey. Let's take you home and hear all about it there, huh?"

CHAPTER 18

Ariadne M. Again

They got her to tell them all about it several times: at home that evening, at the police station the following morning, in an office in City Hall the day after that, and finally, weeks later, in court itself.

Alison enjoyed them all, these sessions of questions and answers, and didn't get bored in the least, even when she had to answer some of the questions ten or more times over. But the occasion she liked the best, even more than the court one with all its publicity, was the second, at the station house, when she and Jeannie and Emmeline were interviewed by a beautiful sandy-haired woman police detective. Particularly did Alison like the last part of this interview when, after she had answered the questions and the young woman had told them the police side of it—about how the Bay Window Woman and her accomplice had been planning the theft for months, and had chosen a Saturday night in the belief that the robbery wouldn't be discovered until Monday, and about how in fact it had been found out on the Sunday afternoon, making the police all the more receptive when they received Emmeline's strange call about Witches and Fetches (via the Hertzes, who were only too glad to pass it on)—the young woman detective then ordered some milk and cookies to be brought in and had relaxed over these refreshments and invited some of *their* questions.

These, after a hesitant start, soon began to flow, brisk and businesslike.

"Are you *really* a lady detective? I mean, not just some kind of a clerk?" (Alison's question. Answer: "Yes. A real detective, give or take a little on the 'lady' bit.")

"Do you like the job?" (Emmeline's question. Answer: "Yes. Love it. But don't tell any of the guys back there or they might ask me to work more extra hours than ever.")

"Do you have any handcuffs?" (Jeannie's question. Answer: "Sure. Pass me that pocketbook and I'll show you.")

"Gee! How d'you get to *be* a lady detective?" (Emmeline's question. Answer: "Work hard at school, look after your health, be prepared to work your way up through boring desk assignments.")

"Please may I try—I mean, will you lock them on *me?*" (Jeannie's question. Answer: No words, just a smile, and *click! click!*)

"Good! Now throw away the keys, Miss—did you say Morrison? Miss Morrison?" (Alison's question. Answer: "Yes, but you can call me Angie if you like.")

"*All of us?*" (Jeannie's and Emmeline's question. Answer: "Why not? That's what your mother always calls me, Jeannie, Alison.")

"*Our* mother?" (Alison's and Jeannie's question. Answer: "Yes. Beth McNair *is* your mother, isn't she?")

"Sure, but how do you know *her?* She—*she hasn't been in trouble with the police, has she?*" (Alison's question. Answer: "Of course not. No. We belong to the same health club. Didn't she tell you? . . . No? . . . Oh, well—we do. In fact, you want to know something? . . . You spent your summer vacation in West Salem, up in Westchester County. Right?")

Here both red heads were nodded vigorously, while Emmeline looked enviously on.

"How—how did you know?" asked Alison.

"Because *you* mentioned it just now," said Emmeline. "When you were talking about the cat."

"Nuh-mm!" said Angie Morrison, shaking her head, her eyes sparkling. "I knew before that. Long before that. I knew as long ago as last June."

"*How?*"

"Because I was the one who recommended the place to your mother. She said that because of something connected with your father's business you needed a place within easy reach of the city this year. Well, I knew just the spot. The house belongs to an old family friend—a friend of *my* mother's."

"And that was it?"

"And that was it. Say, how did you like it there?"

"Oh, well—" began Jeannie.

"At first it was awful," Alison cut in. "But that was only because we had the measles. Then it got better."

"When we became witches—"

Blushing, Alison gave her sister a nudge.

"Witches?" Angie Morrison looked startled, then laughed. "*That* takes me back! Once—when I wasn't much older than you, Alison, Emmeline—my own family took a vacation there. *I* didn't have measles, but it was one of the worst summers on record. Rain, rain, rain. And I remember I found an old Witch Book and spent the rest of my time trying to learn how to be one. . . . Why, what's the matter, Alison?"

"A—an old Witch Book with names in it? *Ariadne M.* and—"

"Ha! Yes! And no! There was only one name written in it when I found it. Frieda or Freddie or something. The other—well, that came later."

"You mean *you*—?"

"*I* wrote that name. Yes. Ariadne M."

"In green ink?"

"I don't remember that much. Could have been."

"But your name is Angie," said Emmeline.

"That was her *ordinary* name," said Alison scornfully. "Ariadne was—well, it must have been your Witch Name, Angie. Wasn't it?"

"Right."

"And you—are you still—I mean—"

"Am I still a witch?" Angie laughed. "I guess not, no."

Jeannie said:

"Was Grouch there when you were there? Mr. Crowther. The garden man."

"Yes, yes. I'm glad you've reminded me of him, honey. . . . Hey, and hold out your hands and let me unlock you before I forget *that!* . . . Yes." Angie straightened up and slipped the handcuffs back into the pocketbook. "Old Rick Crowther. I used to borrow his broom. Now *him* I wouldn't like to tangle with, witchwise. *He*—well—there was something about him that made me feel he knew everything that went on in that house and garden. Especially that garden."

And there the interview came to an end, for, at that point, Angie Morrison was called away by the Emergency Services Section to deal with a woman who was threatening to jump off a thirty-story building—"And we'll need you to use all your charms to talk her out of it," said the lieutenant who'd brought in the message.

But already that session had helped settle Alison's future.

That night, after she'd watched her new heroine successfully tackle this latest assignment—her old faceless green-ink heroine who'd now become a new and living heroine, recognizable even in the blurred TV pictures—Alison made a final entry in her Magical Workbook:

And so—with Norton sitting up on my lap and licking my left cheek as I write—I say Farewell to my Necklace and Thurible, my Garter, my Cord, and my Athamé. Real evil witches to fight and to combat (and lick) there may or may not be, these days (apart from two or three every here and there). But sure as anything there is no shortage of evil ordinaries to fight and combat and lick—thieves and kidnapers and killers—and that is now what shall be my Path. To become a Lady Detective like Angie Morrison, though even better because I shall start in right away (with Emmeline as my rather dumb but trustworthy assistant) by being a GIRL detective—

Alison looked this over for a minute or so, conscious of a momentous hush in the air around her, between the traffic boom outside and the purring in her left ear. She touched noses with Norton, as if for inspiration. Then she added one more phrase to round the whole thing off to her satisfaction:

—a Top-Flight Fully-Automated Junior High School Girl Detective.